The Defense Rests

Craig A. Horowitz

D1520400

"But the Spirit of the Lord came upon Gideon, and he blew a trumpet"
Judges 6:34

PROLOGUE

LANGA Township, South Africa, March 1985

It had been scarcely nine months since Gideon Brown had graduated with honors from the Ivy League. He had decided to take a year off before going to law school. He had already been accepted at Harvard. Gideon knew long ago that he would eventually become a lawyer. His father was a prominent criminal defense attorney who proudly named his only son Gideon after Clarence Earl Gideon, the indigent prisoner who had successfully petitioned the United States Supreme Court to overturn his conviction for petty larceny because he was not provided the assistance of counsel. Gideon Brown was born May 18, 1963, two months to the day after the Supreme Court had announced its historic decision in Gideon v. Wainwright.

Gideon followed in the liberal tradition of his father. When he was in third grade, he campaigned with his father for McGovern. He had demonstrated in front of nuclear power plants. And he had decided to protest apartheid in his year off before law school in South Africa.

Gideon went to South Africa ostensibly to stay with a white family in Johannesburg. Gideon spent most of his time touring the black townships, areas that most whites in South Africa had never ventured into. Gideon could not fathom how, in a matter of miles, such incredible opulence and wealth displayed in white communities could turn into the squalor and poverty that pervaded the black townships.

1

It was during the tours of the black townships that Gideon befriended a family in Langa township outside of Vitenhage, located on the Eastern Cape, an area long regarded as troublesome by the authorities and which was suffering from the worst effects of the recession. Unemployment in the port Elizabeth-Vitenhage area, the location of much of South African's automobile industry, was over 50%. The black slums were noted for their extreme poverty.

Gideon had taken part in several protests against the rising cost of living and mass unemployment. Then, on March 21, 1985, an event occurred which would create an indelible mark on Gideon. He was attending a funeral of a friend of the family with whom he had struck up a relationship. On the way to the funeral, armed police in two armored vehicles without warning opened fire on the procession of blacks headed to the funeral. Gideon was not hit. The family Gideon was with was not so lucky. The mother was struck by a bullet and killed instantly. Gideon watched her die in the street. In all, twenty black Africans were massacred in Langa township that day, many of them as they tried to flee.

Gideon vowed to use his law degree, the day that President Botha declared a state of emergency in thirty-six magisterial districts in the Eastern Cape, the East Rand, the Vaal triangle and Johannesburg.

Part I

1

The day began for Gideon like most other Mondays during the past five years. It had been that long since he had started practicing law for Longworth & Drucker, the premier Los Angeles law firm. His alarm went off louder than necessary at 7:00 a.m. He flicked the switch on the radio to off and put his head back on the pillow. He dozed until about 7:30 a.m.

At 7:30, Gideon leapt out of bed and began his frenetic routine as he readied himself for work. He jumped into the shower for about a minute. He ran his razor over his face too quickly to shave close, but enough to rid himself of most of his perennial five o'clock shadow. He picked out a suit and shirt from the closet and started at the tie rack. He removed an abstract tie, placed it around his neck and tied it a touch too long and slightly off center. He gave his half-asleep wife a peck on the cheek and headed out the door. It was 7:50 a.m.

The commute to work was barely over ten miles, yet, depending on traffic, it took between thirty and forty minutes. The traffic was bumper-to-bumper on this sunny summer morning and Gideon settled back in the seat of his red sports car knowing he would once again begin the day later than hoped.

He arrived in the office at 8:30 a.m. As usual, the message

light on his phone was flashing, meaning that either clients or other lawyers had already tried to reach him. He took off his jacket, turned on the speaker phone and pushed the message waiting button. He heard the dreaded, "You have four new messages. To hear your messages, press 1." Gideon did so.

The first call was from a lawyer in the New York office requesting a copy of a brief Gideon had done about a year ago in a case involving the termination of an employee by an employer for insubordination. He saved the message and promised himself that he would respond to it later. The second message was not any more interesting. A partner wanted to know if anybody had information about the reputation of an opposing lawyer representing a plaintiff in a new case that he had just received from a new client. The name of the plaintiff's lawyer was completely unfamiliar to Gideon and he erased the message. The third message was from one of Gideon favorite clients, Bill Stevens, the director of personnel of a plastics manufacturer outside of Los Angeles. Stevens and Gideon spoke on an almost daily basis about personnel issues that arose in his workforce. In the past couple of years, Gideon had done half a dozen arbitrations for Stevens on a variety of issues, ranging from employee to interpretation of language in the contract that the company held with its union.

Gideon was about to return the call when he heard his fourth message. It was from the same partner who left the message regarding the reputation of an opposing lawyer in a new case. E. Barton

4

McCabe, the partner, wanted Gideon to see him as soon as he came into the office. McCabe had a new case that he wanted Gideon to start on immediately. Gideon enjoyed working for McCabe, one of the more senior partners in the law firm and head of the firm's labor department. McCabe had a wide array of clients and he spent most of his time bringing in new business and keeping clients entertained. He was a brilliant lawyer with a keen memory. Gideon was always astonished that McCabe could keep track of all the various cases he supervised. McCabe would rarely get involved in day-to-day decisions, but he reviewed major briefs that Gideon wrote and, on occasion, attend a client meeting. Otherwise he gave Gideon free reign on his cases, which Gideon enjoyed.

Indeed, McCabe was one of the reasons Gideon had stayed with Longworth & Drucker so long. Gideon had come to work with Longworth & Drucker almost by accident. After his first two years of law school, Gideon worked for the legal clinics helping the poor while his classmates all worked at large firms. As much as he despised the corporate culture, he recognized that his classmates were receiving superb legal training. Gideon felt that spending a year or two in an established law firm would season him as a lawyer and open the door to other areas – perhaps politics. On a lark, Gideon applied during his third year for a position with Longworth & Drucker. Much to his surprise, he received an offer even though he felt he did not fit into the L&D mold – workaholic, totally devoted to the firm, with family a distant second to the job. Gideon talked about the offer with his father, who agreed that it was tough to turn down an offer from the best firm in town. It would pay $70,000 the first year. Gideon took it. Five years later, with a salary well in excess of six figures, he was still there.

Gideon grabbed a cup of coffee on his way to McCabe's office. The door was shut. Gideon knocked on the door and peeked in. McCabe, as usual, was on the phone but waved Gideon into the office. McCabe's phone conversation continued as Gideon sat and waited. McCabe had yet to make eye contact with Gideon when he pushed a document in front of him. Gideon glanced down and immediately recognized it as a Summons and Complaint filed in Superior Court in Los Angeles. He had seen dozens of similar documents during his five years with Longworth & Drucker. A Complaint is a legal document filed by an individual suing another which commences the lawsuit. This particular Complaint looked no different than most others. It involved an individual named Jerry Morgan. The defendant was a company called Western Health Corp.

Gideon was vaguely familiar with the company. It was a company that had made the news in the past several years because of a dramatic increase in the price of its stock. The company had developed several new prescription type drugs which had gotten FDA approval and were widely prescribed by physicians. One of the drugs, Marvil, was hailed as a major breakthrough in the treatment of depression. Unlike other drugs of this type, it had no apparent side effects – not even drowsiness. Morgan claimed in the Complaint

6

that Western Health Corp. had fired him because he was concerned about the safety of Marvil. McCabe finished his phone call and faced Gideon for the first time. Without exchanging a hello or good morning, McCabe launched right into the task in store for Gideon.

"We just got this Complaint in last night," McCabe began. "For several months, we have been engaged in a beauty contest with several other law firms for Western Health Corp.'s business. This case has been expected for some time and they have aggressively interviewed the best law firms in Los Angeles. They decided to take us based on our experience in whistle blower cases. I promised to staff the case lean and to keep junior attorney and paralegal involvement to a minimum. That doesn't mean we can cut any corners, and the company expects that its bills will be substantial. They know your time will be billed at $250 per hour. They know this case will cost them several hundred thousand dollars in legal fees. They just want one person who will know all facets of this case who they can call at any time with any questions that they have. While I'll be overseeing this case, I want you to take this case and run with it. If you do a good job for them, I'll recommend that you do the trial."

Gideon had heard all of this many times before. Every new case that came in the door was treated with a sense of urgency. Although 99% of the cases the firm handled eventually were dismissed or settled before trial, the initial conversations were such that it seemed given that the case would go to trial. In fact, in the five years that Gideon had been at the firm, he had only been involved in one jury trial, and the entire labor department, which had over 40 attorneys, had only done a handful of others. Still, he liked the idea of working on a new case for a new client. The firm had increasingly stressed the importance of associates developing a client base, and this seemed like a perfect opportunity for him to get to know a new client and try to develop more business. He also knew that if he won such a high-profile case, he would be in for a huge bonus and he would enhance his partnership prospects – a decision the firm would make in less than one year.

Gideon responded to McCabe's speech enthusiastically. "Sounds great to me, Bart," Gideon said. "I'll make this case my first priority. Who shall I call out there in order to set up interviews?" "The president of the company is named Ted Greene," McCabe said. "Greene is expecting a phone call from us this morning. I'd like to introduce you to Greene by phone and then let you run with it from there. Greene may want you to come out today to meet the plaintiff's supervisor and to meet the other key players. He is very anxious to get this under way. Do you have anything scheduled today?"

Gideon had planned to write a brief that was due later in the week and knew that his client Bill Stevens needed to discuss some issues with him. He had also promised his wife he would be home by 7:30 p.m. and help complete a few small projects that they had been working on around the house the past weekend.

Yet, there was only one response to McCabe's rhetorical question. "Should be no problem, Bart," Gideon offered with the requisite enthusiasm, "I'll make a couple phone calls to rearrange things and then I can go out to the company whenever they want me."

McCabe had his secretary place the call to Greene. While they were waiting for the call to come through, McCabe described the company in more detail. "Greene is a young guy to be president of such a successful company. He graduated business school at 24. He began his career marketing medical supplies and quickly worked his way up the ladder. He got into Western Health Corp. on the ground floor, and it was his aggressive marketing approach that quickly led him up the ranks. He became president of the company at age 36, and it's been his leadership in the last five years that has propelled the company to where it's at. He is a good businessman, but a likable guy, and I think he'll make an excellent witness." Gideon also heard those words before. No one would ever dare say that the company president – the person paying the bills – would make a miserable witness. Yet, time and time again, when cases went to trial, the jury received an unfavorable impression from testimony of top company executives. Too often, the witness seemed aloof and removed from the situation and the jury knew it. Hopefully, Greene would be different.

McCabe's phone buzzed, and he depressed the speakerphone. Gideon heard McCabe's secretary say that Ted Greene was on the line and put Greene through. Greene wasted no time getting to the point. "Bart, I've been expecting your call. Have you had a chance to review the Complaint yet? What do you think about this case?"

McCabe responded in a measured, yet reassuring way. "The Complaint is pretty vague, and we think there are significant legal defenses to this lawsuit. We are prepared to run with this one. Before we take any depositions, or make any motions, we need to talk to some of the key players. I've got Gideon Brown in my office, Ted, and he's going to help me on this case. He's very experienced in these types of cases, and I think it would be good if he got out to your place as soon as possible to interview those who had any dealings with the plaintiff."

Greene liked what he heard. "That sounds fine, Bart. I'll tell you; I want to move as quickly as we can in this case."

"This case is going to get a lot of publicity and it can do nothing but hurt our stock. I want to either get rid of it by motion or try it soon."

McCabe immediately responded. "Ted, we're ready to roll on this today if necessary. When do you want Gideon to come out to the company?" Greene said he would line up witnesses for meetings to begin at 1:00 p.m. McCabe said that Gideon would be there, and the conversation concluded. By the time the conversation ended it was 9:30 a.m. The company was located in a nearby suburb of L.A. But with traffic it could take an hour to an hour and a half. Gideon knew that he would have to do some preliminary work before going out to the company. Before he told McCabe what his plans were, McCabe gave him the litany of things to do.

"Go to the computer and pull up all the articles about Western

Health Corp. in the last two years. I want you to be familiar with the company and what's been happening there when you go out to see Greene and the witnesses. Make a good impression. This case could lead to a lot of new business."

Gideon did not need to be reminded how important it was to win. He hated to lose. And winning had always been an overriding passion. Perhaps it was because, as the youngest of three boys, he always strived to keep up with the accomplishments of his brothers. His oldest brother was the valedictorian of his high school class; he was now a successful doctor. The middle brother was the sports maniac who now was a partner in an engineering firm. Gideon had a lot to live up to.

Before McCabe finished the sentence, his phone rang, and he was busy on another call. He motioned Gideon out the door, put his hand over the phone, and asked Gideon to leave a message about the day's interviews when he returned. Gideon spent the next two hours in the library brushing up on Western Health Corp. He jumped in the car at 11:30 a.m., more than enough time to make it by 1:00 p.m. for the interviews. He had forgotten to call back his client Bill Stevens or to let his wife know that he might be late getting home.

2

The third-story apartment faced to the north. It was dingy and never received direct sunlight. It was a one-room setup, commonly called a bachelor apartment. The living room served as a bedroom; there was a mattress on the floor in the middle of the room. The alarm went off at 10:00 a.m. He barely moved in response. It had been another night of partying until the wee hours. He had somehow made it back to the apartment and passed out about 3:00 a.m. He had set the alarm because he had an appointment – a very important one.

He eased himself off the floor and back to the bathroom. He made his way into the shower stall and turned on the water. It was ice cold as usual. Damn it, he thought to himself, he had to get out of this rat hole. There is only one sure fire way to do so. He put on some wrinkled clothes and headed out of the apartment. He got in his car and drove across town. Rather than leaving the car with the parking attendant, he drove around the block to find an open space. He found one about two blocks from his destination.

He walked into the building and took an elevator up to the second floor. He walked to the reception desk and cleared his throat. "Jerry Morgan to see Bill Jacobs. We have an appointment." "You're late again, Mr. Morgan. The appointment was for 10:30 sharp. Do you know what time it is?" Morgan looked at his watch and saw that it was nearly 11:30. "Mr. Jacobs is not pleased. But go back there anyway."

Morgan found his way back to Jacobs' office. He had piles of paper on his desk and looked extremely busy. Jacobs glared at Morgan as he stepped into the office. "Jerry, I'm not going to put up with this anymore. I've told you that if you want me to help you in this case, you've got to get your act together. You have got to stop partying. You've got to look presentable. You've got to get yourself a haircut and some new clothes. Now what's it going to be? I'm ready to drop this case today." Morgan knew that Jacobs was right. "I just got a little out of control last night, Bill. It won't happen again." "Listen," Jacobs said, "things are going to happen quickly now. The Complaint has been filed. We know that Western Health Corp. will have some fancy law firm defending them in an aggressive fashion. If they see you looking like this, they'll make mincemeat out of you. It'll be embarrassing."

Jacobs reached into his pocket and took out five crisp $100 bills. "Here, take this. Get your ass down to the garment district and get a new suit. Get a tie, too. Get your damned haircut. Next time I see you, I want to see Jerry Morgan, clean cut, ex-Western Health Corp. employee. I want that look of confidence. I don't want to see an unemployed bum near the brink. Now get the hell out of here."

3

The traffic was bumper-to-bumper to Western Health Corp. If Gideon had any quirk, he always left ample time to make any appointment – social or business – because of his disdain for being late and because of his woeful sense of direction. He could always count on making at least a wrong turn or two in the course of any trip. This trip was no different. He did fine until he got off the exit of the freeway, then promptly turned the wrong way and went two miles before realizing the mistake. He backtracked and eventually found his way, arriving just at 1:00 p.m. He had hoped to make it out to the company with a little time to spare so that he could catch a bit at a fast food joint before beginning the meetings. Lunch would have to wait.

Gideon entered the lobby of the sleek three-story, ultra-modern building. It was apparent that the occupant of the building had come into recent money – everything inside was brand new. The art collection in the lobby was contemporary and striking. He thought to himself that his wife would approve of the selection. Gideon's wife, Ali (short for Alison), was an interior decorator and a fledgling artist. The more abstract the art the better Ali liked it.

She did quite well, given Los Angeles' penchant for something new and different. Gideon had actually learned a lot about contemporary art and had grown to enjoy it since he had met Ali some three years earlier.

Gideon approached the receptionist and informed her that he was present for a 1:00 p.m. meeting with Ted Greene. Gideon took a seat and was almost immediately greeted by Greene's secretary. He was led to the elevator and taken to the third floor. Greene's secretary was attractive, talkative and friendly. "Ted's been expecting you. He really is anxious about this case. The whole company is buzzing about it." Gideon assured Greene's secretary that he was there to do all he could for Greene and the company, as if she was the person he needed to impress. He was decidedly nervous as he stepped out of the elevator and headed behind her toward Greene's office.

Gideon had learned the hard way how important it was to make a good first impression. In the seventh grade he was one of 50 boys who tried out for the junior high basketball team. Most were tall. Gideon did not look like a player. He was a short, very frail, Jewish kid. But he could play. And shoot.

Gideon got lost in the shuffle in the three-day tryout. Each kid had very little court time. He was convinced the coach did not even see him touch the ball. He was cut from the team. Gideon was devastated. His brother convinced him to talk to the coach. Ask for a second chance. He told Gideon to come to practice. Gideon promised not to complain if the coach decided to cut him after taking another look.

Gideon came to practice possessed. He ran faster and harder than anyone. He made his shots. He dove after balls.

He stole the ball on defense. He was invited to continue coming to practice. Gideon made the team. Word got around. Rumors spread that Gideon cried his way back on the team. Gideon tried to ignore the taunts.

One day Gideon was outside the school during lunch. A huge kid who had been cut from the team came up and started pushing him. Gideon stood his ground. Words were exchanged. A large switchblade then became the focus of attention. "I should cut you for crying your way back to the team," the huge kid shouted at Gideon. Gideon did not flinch. More words were exchanged. The knife was finally put away.

Gideon not only made the team, but he was in the starting lineup in the first game. He was the only kid under six feet tall out there, and it would turn out to be the best game of his high school basketball career. His team lost but he was the game's high scorer. Gideon did not cry to make the team. And he does not remember ever crying since.

None of this was consciously in Gideon's mind as he entered Greene's office.

Greene had a corner office with a beautiful view of the surrounding mountains. It was much more spacious than even the most senior partner's office at Longworth & Drucker. Greene's desk was strikingly modern – an all glass top with a black metal base in the shape of a large ball. His desk was neat and organized with various piles of papers at seemingly measured intervals.

Gideon walked up to Greene and introduced himself. "Pleasure to meet you, Mr. Greene, I'm Gideon Brown and I'm looking forward to working with you on this case." Greene stood up and shook Gideon's hand. Greene was tall, probably 6'1" or 6'2", and quite fit. It was clear that he worked out regularly. He had black hair and was clean shaven, making him look even younger than McCabe had described to him. He wore a European tailored suit that probably cost ten times what Gideon spent on one of his suits. He was handsome and well-groomed. There was no doubt in Gideon's mind that a jury would immediately find him appealing.

"Call me Ted, everybody in the company does. Let's chat for a little about the case and then I will take you to meet Alex Benczik, the chemist who was directly involved in the FDA procedures involving Marvil. Your last interview will be with Ben Williams who was Morgan's direct supervisor."

Gideon took a seat and asked Greene if he would give him a little background about the Morgan case. It was soon clear to Gideon that Greene was no novice in this type of litigation. "Frankly," Greene began, "I suspected that Morgan would be the type of person to sue the company. We've had a couple of problem employees in the past and have been involved in a few wrongful discharge lawsuits. None of them amounted to much and we were able to settle them or get them dismissed before trial. This one worries me, however. Morgan is making serious allegations of the safety of Marvil, and although we know that Marvil is completely safe, it's going to be our word against his. And he might have a jury's sympathy if it gets that far."

"One of the things we'll find out in his deposition is how he came about the information he claims to have discovered regarding Marvil," Gideon told Greene. "Morgan is not a chemist, and we will try to establish that, as a marketing person, he simply was not involved in the FDA procedures and that any information he has is based on pure speculation or conjecture. If that is the case, we may have a chance of getting this case knocked out on a summary judgment motion." What Gideon was referring to is a motion commonly filed by defense counsel prior to trial to try to dismiss a case before it reaches a jury. "I know I'll be talking to his supervisor," Gideon continued, "but why don't you tell me a little bit about the company and about Morgan's responsibilities?"

Greene began to describe the structure of the company. The company had three separate departments: marketing, laboratory and management. Its marketing staff, among them Morgan, were the persons who were directly involved in selling Western Health Corp.'s products. They dealt not only with pharmacies, but also with physicians who might prescribe the various drugs. They also were in charge of advertising and had developed some aggressive TV and radio spots that made Western Health Corp. a household name.

Morgan was a fairly low-level employee, having been at the company only five years. He had been a steady performer and had kept up with others in his department with respect to sales. However, in the six months prior to his dismissal, his productivity declined sharply. He seemed preoccupied, arrived to work late on a frequent basis, and refused to follow instructions of his supervisor. He was warned in writing about his conduct and told that if he did not improve, he would have to be let go. Rather than heeding the warning, his performance got worse, and he was eventually dismissed from employment. It was not until after his dismissal that Morgan began complaining to the company that their new drug Marvil was dangerous. Greene stated unequivocally that when he authorized Morgan's dismissal, he had no idea that Morgan was alleging that Marvil was a dangerous drug.

"What you need to know," Greene continued, "is that this company is run like a small operation, even though we have expanded significantly over the last several years. No employment decision is made without my approval. Ben Williams, Morgan's supervisor, kept me apprised about all aspects of Morgan's employment, and we developed a specific strategy to try to improve his performance and avoid termination. We thought that Morgan would calm down when he got the warning and just do his job. He just never picked up his productivity."

Gideon took detailed notes as Greene continued the description of the case. "If I had any clue that Morgan would make such allegations, I obviously would not have terminated him and would have investigated this internally and disproved his allegations. Unfortunately, it seems like he has drummed all of this up to try to make a big deal out of nothing and ruin the company."

Gideon asked Greene to describe the procedures involved in getting FDA approval for Marvil. Greene told Gideon that Alex Benczik, the chemist, was the best source for that information, but described the process in general terms. "To begin with, it's simply preposterous for Morgan to claim that Marvil is unsafe when the FDA just a year ago examined all our records, did its own tests, and concluded that the drug was completely safe for human consumption. Every psychiatrist who has prescribed Marvil has marveled about the drug's effect in treating depression without any major side-effects. It truly is a drug that has revolutionized the treatment of depression, and obviously the financial analysts agree, given that our stock has increased threefold since we put the drug on the market nine months ago. We opened all our books to the FDA, and I will have copies made of all the documents so that you have them for your file. They are voluminous, but I am sure that at some point the other side is going to request to review them, and I want you to be familiar with them before you turn them over."

Gideon told Greene that he indeed would want to review all the documents as soon as possible. Greene told Gideon he would have his secretary make copies of all the files within the next several days and have them shipped down to Gideon's office. Greene warned

Gideon that the documents, which were all in his locked file cabinet in the office, would probably fill about ten boxes. Greene then asked Gideon if he could advise what would occur in the lawsuit in the next several months.

Gideon told Greene that after completing the interviews scheduled for the day, he would prepare what is called an Answer to the Complaint filed by Morgan. An Answer is the first document filed in court by someone being sued and is pretty much boilerplate. Gideon could ship out an Answer within a day or two and get it filed. He also told Greene that at the time he filed the Answer, he would send out a notice setting a date for Morgan's deposition, as well as a request that Morgan bring all documents in his possession relevant to the lawsuit to the deposition. A deposition is a procedure that takes place before trial, at which the lawyer asks the witness certain questions. A court reporter attends the deposition and transcribes all the questions and answers into a booklet form. The purpose of the deposition is for the lawyer to learn what the witness plans to testify about at trial and to get admissions from the witness that might be helpful in pre-trial motions.

Gideon knew that Greene had been through this procedure before, since he nodded affirmatively and was not surprised by any of the information that Gideon was sharing with him. "I will need to have one of the representatives present at the deposition in case I have any questions," Gideon said. "I don't think it's necessary for you to be there, given that the deposition may go for some time. I would suggest that we send Morgan's immediate supervisor, who is familiar with the terminology and can give me some insight into Morgan's testimony." Greene agreed and said that Williams would be available whenever Gideon needed him to attend the deposition and to do anything else necessary.

Gideon and Greene exchanged pleasantries and discussed the upcoming Dodger series at home against the Braves. Gideon mentioned to Greene that before long they could meet and go to a Dodger game in the firm seats.

Greene said he would love to do so, and that he would bring his wife. Gideon told Greene that he would see what tickets were available when he returned to the firm the next day and arrange for tickets for a game in the near future. Gideon was pleased that he had found a common interest with Greene and that they seemed to hit it off well. He was feeling more comfortable about the case.

By the time Gideon had finished his interview with Greene, it was nearly three o'clock. Greene led Gideon to a large conference room down the hallway, introduced him to Alex Benczik and departed. Gideon shook Benczik's hand, and the two began idle chit-chat. "Ted seems like a great guy to work for," Gideon offered. Benczik immediately agreed. "You would hardly know he's a multi-millionaire from the way he treats his employees. He's really a hands-on guy – he knows everything that's going on in this company. There's not a single employee who can't knock on his door and walk into his office and ask him anything. It's one of the reasons that I'm still at the company."

Benczik looked exactly like what one would think a chemist looked like. He was thin and graying. He wore large, dark rimmed glasses and a white lab coat. He had clearly been doing some work in the laboratory before coming over for the meeting. Gideon felt that a jury would think that Benczik was extremely smart, which is good for a chemist-type. He was well spoken and appeared very competent. A jury would immediately pick up on this, Gideon thought to himself. Gideon asked Benczik to run him through the basics – what Marvil was used for, how it was created and the process by which the FDA approved the drug. Gideon realized that this would all get very complicated and that he would need to talk with Benczik at much greater length during the course of the litigation. In the meantime, Gideon simply wanted to get as much information about the drug as possible.

Benczik had been the person responsible for developing the drug which would become known nationwide as Marvil. He had spent years in the lab trying to develop a drug that would be effective in treating depression and which had no major side effects. He had come up with the compound and had tested the drug on laboratory mice. Much to his surprise, the mice exhibited none of the side effects typical of antidepressant drugs, such as drowsiness, loss of appetite, or lack of sexual drive. He had tested the laboratory mice for a number of diseases, and none were found. Greene was especially anxious to get the drug on the market and worked closely with Benczik during the FDA procedures. The FDA approved of Marvil in record time.

Gideon asked Benczik if he had any documents regarding the FDA procedures. Benczik told him that all the documents regarding the testing and FDA approval of Marvil were in Greene's office, and that Greene would provide these documents to him.

Benczik actually knew very little about Morgan and what he did at the company. He had met him on a number of occasions at company social events but had little contact on a day-to-day basis. They were in different departments and Benczik assured Gideon that Morgan had nothing to do with the FDA approval of Marvil and knew absolutely nothing about the drug, other than what he needed to know for marketing purposes. Benczik could not think of anybody at the company who Morgan could possibly have spoken to regarding the drug. He had never seen Morgan in the lab or anywhere near any of the documentation regarding Marvil. It was nearly four o'clock by the time Gideon completed his interview with Benczik.

Benczik had been told to take Gideon to Ben Williams' office after his interview was completed. Gideon had still not had a chance to grab anything to eat and had not even gone to the bathroom since he had arrived in the office at 8:30 that morning. He made a quick stop in the restroom, and then proceeded with Benczik to see Williams.

Williams' official title was Director of Marketing. He was responsible for overseeing the marketing efforts of the hundred or so employees doing marketing work for Western Health Corp. Williams had been with the company since its inception. He had begun as a marketing agent and had worked his way up to supervise the entire department. It was obvious he was prepared to meet with Gideon, as he had Morgan's entire personnel file on his desk and began going over it with Gideon. He had clearly been through this before.

During the next two and a half hours, Williams went through page-by-page of Morgan's personnel file. Gideon barely had a chance to intervene and ask any questions. Williams had done an unbelievably thorough job in documenting all discipline issued against Morgan, as well as prepared comprehensive performance reviews. He went line-by-line through each and every review that he had prepared on Morgan during his five years at the company.

Unlike many of the performance reviews that Gideon has seen in the past, they were candid and to the point about performance deficiencies, as well as strong areas of performance. Gideon was pleased to find out that he would not be faced with trying a case involving an employee who had all performance evaluations until the time he was terminated. Gideon felt that Williams was a bit verbose, but that a jury would conclude that he would not make a rash decision with respect to terminating an employee.

By the time they had gone through the personnel file, it was nearly 6:30 p.m. Williams suggested that they go to a nearby restaurant to catch a quick dinner, and then complete the conversation. Gideon agreed, but before he had a chance to use the phone to call his wife, he was whisked to the elevator and outside to a nearby restaurant. Williams and Gideon continued to talk about Morgan over some pasta and a bottle of red wine.

"From the day I met Morgan, I just felt that there was something odd about him," Williams said. "He was one of these hyperactive guys. He would come in the office and immediately get down to business. He would make more cold calls than anyone else in the office. We always rated him highly on productivity and initiative, but we were always concerned about his knowledge of the product, his relations with customers, his thoroughness. Sometimes he seemed to be in another world."

None of this struck Gideon as being incredibly important. It was pretty common for supervisors to bad mouth employees once they had been terminated. Still, Gideon felt that there was something sincere about Williams' response and that he honestly felt that there was something strange about Morgan. He vowed to look through all the documents with great care to see if they would cast any light on what Williams was telling him.

The two finished their dinner and returned to the office. Williams gave Gideon a bit more detail on Morgan's job duties and his employment history. By the time Gideon left Williams' office, it was 9:00 p.m. He was already on the freeway by the time he realized that he had not yet called Ali to tell her he would be late. His cell phone was dead, and he was too tired to get off the freeway to make the call.

He arrived at the house at 10:00 p.m. The automatic sprinklers were on, and Gideon sprinted to the house to avoid getting wet. The house was dark. Ali had already gone to bed. There was some pasta on the stove that was still warm. Gideon took the pot, put a piece of foil over it, and replaced it in the refrigerator. Ali was only half asleep, but he could tell that she was in no mood to talk with him. He took off his clothes and went out back to the hot tub. He took a long Jacuzzi and then read in the living room for about an hour. He felt right to sleep when he put his head on the pillow at about 11:30 that night.

4

The light was still on in Jacobs' office. As a solo practitioner, Jacobs frequently found himself in the office until the early morning hours. It wasn't that he was so busy and successful. It was more just attempting to keep his head above water and scramble to make a buck. The Morgan case would clearly be the biggest case he had ever handled. The rest of his practice was catch-as-catch can: some personal injury work, some wills, some contracts, anything to pay the rent.

This was the second career for Jacobs. He had graduated college and gone into the pharmacy business. He found the work dull. In his spare time, he had gone to law school at night. It took him four, instead of three, years to graduate. However, he passed the California Bar exam the first time.

He had taken on the Morgan case as a favor. He had met the Morgan family while in the pharmacy business. Jerry Morgan's mother was a diabetic, who had been in and out of hospitals for years. Jerry's father frequently came in the pharmacy to get medicine. Jacobs and Jack Morgan had become friendly. The Morgans were good people who had lived through some hard times.

Jack Morgan was an extremely successful businessman. He

had made a mint in the commercial real estate boom in California in the 70's and 80's. He had also borne much of the responsibility for raising the Morgan children. His two older daughters had been model students and children. Both were married and had started their own families.

The youngest, Jerry, had always been a problem. Although Jacobs did not know the specifics, he knew that Jerry had a wild streak, and had disappointed his father a number of times.

Thus, when Jack Morgan strolled into Jacobs' office several months earlier, Jacobs could not turn down his request. The one problem was money. Plaintiff's lawyers generally work on a contingency basis – meaning no money unless you win. Jacobs simply couldn't afford to bankroll a case. Jack Morgan was understanding. He agreed to give Jacobs a $20,000 non-refundable retainer. If Jacobs lost the case, at least he would get $20,000. If he won, he would also get a share of the judgment.

It was a difficult case to handle. Jack Morgan and his son Jerry were estranged. They had not spoken in several years. Jack had decided that he would no longer offer any financial support to Jerry. That is why Jacobs felt compelled to use part of the retainer to try to make Jerry look presentable. Despite the fact that the Morgans did not speak, Jack felt that Jerry had been given a bum deal by Western Health Corp. He knew his son probably wasn't the model employee, but he had his moments. He had been in business a long time and knew that you just didn't fire an employee so suddenly unless something fishy was going on. He felt his son had probably stuck his nose into something which the bigwigs at Western Health Corp. didn't appreciate. He thought that Jacobs, his longtime friend, might be able to make something of the case. His pharmaceutical background couldn't hurt either.

Jacobs shared Jack Morgan's suspicions, but he had very little tangible to go on. Jerry Morgan had given him a number of documents to review, but none gave him any useful leads. He knew that Jerry would have surprise testimony that could cast some suspicion on Western Health Corp., but he did not know whether it would be enough to carry the day. The key would be to try to get some Western Health Corp. employee in the know to help out on the case. Jacobs was not sure at this point who that person would be and how he would get such assistance. He would have to access the witnesses as they came long, to see if there was an easy touch.

5

As usual, Gideon arrived in the office the following day at 8:30 a.m. He cringed as he saw the red message light flashing on his telephone. There was only one message. It was from McCabe. "What the hell happened in the meeting?" McCabe said. "Get down to my office as soon as you get in." There was also a note on his desk scribbled in pencil as usual, which simply stated, "Please see me." That was McCabe's trademark, and all the associates knew it. Gideon grabbed a cup of coffee and headed down to McCabe's office. He had completely forgotten to give McCabe an update as to the prior day's events.

McCabe as on the phone. He waved Gideon in. McCabe finished his phone call and asked Gideon to brief him.

Gideon described the meeting at Western Health Corp. in an upbeat fashion. After two minutes, McCabe interrupted, "Sounds like you've got it under control. Make sure to look at the documents quickly. Let's answer this Complaint and depose the plaintiff. Greene will be happy if we speed this thing along."

Gideon went back to his office and began completing the tasks that were left undone from yesterday. He called Bill Stevens and answered some questions he had about personnel matters. He wrote the brief he had planned to do the day before, working on it through lunch into the early evening. He asked his secretary to stay late and put in the changes, and the brief was completed by about seven that night. He was about to head out the door when his phone rang.

"This is the reception area," the voice began. "We have ten boxes of documents that were hand-delivered by Western Health Corp. Would you like us to bring them down now or do you want them in the morning?" Gideon wanted to answer the latter, but knew that he ought to at least see what was in store for him. "Bring them down now, please. I'll wait for them."

The documents arrived about ten minutes later. Much to Gideon's delight, they were neatly organized under various categories. One box contained a copy of Morgan's personnel file, which he had reviewed with Williams the day before. Two other boxes contained the personnel policies available to Western Health Corp. employees. The remaining documents pertained to Marvil and the FDA review and eventual approval of the drug. Clearly, Western Health Corp. had good staff to have these documents kept in such an organized fashion.

Gideon was again about to head out the door when his phone rang. He thought it was probably Ali asking when he would be home for dinner. Instead it was Ted Greene on the line. "Gideon," Greene began, "I hope you'll be leaving soon, but I just wanted to make sure the documents got there in good shape."

Gideon assured Greene that he had the documents and that

they looked to be in order. Gideon promised Greene that he would go through the documents within the next couple days and give Greene some preliminary ideas about their strategy in defending the lawsuit. Gideon also advised Greene that he might at some point need some of the originals of the documents if the other side asked for them in discovery, or if some of the copies were illegible.

Greene was completely cooperative. "I'll tell you what – I will send you in the mail a set of keys to the office and to the file cabinet where the originals are kept. You don't even need to make an appointment to come up. Anytime you want to look at anything, just let yourself in and help yourself. I want to make the process as easy as possible."

These were the type of words that lawyers only hoped to hear from clients, but rarely did. The document review process in litigation is one of the most arduous of all, one that no lawyer or client likes. Reviewing the documents is tedious, and it is usually a tremendous burden on the client to get all the documents together. There were countless times that Gideon had to get extensions to produce documents, because his clients either could not get them together in time or the documents were so disorganized that it took weeks to make any sense out of them. It appeared to Gideon that this case would be the exception.

"I really appreciate that, Ted. I'll call ahead if I need to come up, but I appreciate your efforts in making the documents available." The two exchanged pleasantries and completed the conversation. It was a little past 7:30 p.m. when Gideon left the office, and shortly after 8:00 p.m. when he arrived home.

Ali was not in a good mood. She was unhappy that Gideon had not told her he would be unable to help her finish the house projects the night before. She was generally good about these things, and Gideon knew that he really just needed to let her vent her displeasure.

Over dinner, the two caught up with each other about the events in the past couple of days. Ali was excited about a new client she had just talked to who wanted to buy some modern photographs for her living room. Ali had a number of contacts in the art business and thought she had just the perfect piece for the living room. She felt that if the client liked the piece, she might use her to remodel other parts of the house. Gideon told Ali about his new case and his meetings at Western Health Corp. Gideon liked to get Ali's reaction about his cases as they proceeded to trial. Ali's responses or views would be much more like the typical juror than the ones he would get in the office.

All lawyers tend to get involved in their cases, and those in his line of work rarely see the facts like a jury would.

Often, Gideon would shape his arguments in court or before a jury based on ideas given to him by Ali. Ali's response to Gideon's description of the case, however, bothered him. "You mean this guy suspected that one of the drugs was dangerous and they fired him? That doesn't sound like a very good case to me, Gideon."

Gideon explained to Ali that no one at the company even knew that Morgan was complaining about the drug when they fired him. "Ali, they fired this guy because he was completely unproductive, they warned him about it and told him he needed to straighten out, but he just got worse. By the end he wasn't even coming to work and was acting very bizarrely."

"What do you think the company is going to tell you?" Ali said to Gideon. "I mean, they're not going to flat out say that they fired this guy because he was complaining about the drug being unsafe. That wouldn't be too smart of them, would it?"

Gideon knew that Ali's reaction was one that he would likely be confronted with by a jury. He realized that he would have to do all he could in discovery to dispel the very thoughts that Ali was expressing. One of the ways he could do that was to come up with an explanation why Morgan, who had been a good employee, suddenly had become unproductive and had acted in the workplace bizarrely. Maybe, Gideon thought to himself, something in the documents would give him some leads in that respect.

By the time the evening had ended, Gideon and Ali had made up. They went to be early and made love. Ali fell asleep shortly afterward, but Gideon's mind was spinning. He didn't fall asleep until well after midnight and the sleep was fitful at best. By around 6:00 a.m., Gideon knew that the best thing was just to get up and go to work and start on the documents. Maybe after he got through some of them, it would put his mind at ease. He kissed Ali goodbye and headed off for another day at the office.

6

As one man's day begins, another man's day often ends. Morgan had used $20 of the $500 given to him by Jacobs to get a haircut. That left $480. It seemed such a waste to spend that on clothes. Surely, the old man would relent and give him some money for that purpose if it meant winning the case. Morgan was confident that the business side of good old Jack would overcome any petty animosity that the old man might have toward him.

With $480 he could be king for a night. He would worry later about the next day. He made a quick phone call and scored some coke. He headed down towards the airport to the all-nude revue.

Morgan had not been with a woman since he was fired from Western Health Corp. He had been too depressed.

But money can build a man's confidence. He sat at the front, near the stage, and ordered a pitcher of beer. He would watch the women strut their stuff. He would decide which one he wanted. A little blow and some bucks would buy him a night to remember.

He watched act after act. Some of the women were attractive, others were way over the hill. At about 2:00 a.m., he saw a woman who caught his fancy. She was petite, with firm breasts and lot of energy. He motioned her to come over to his spot by the stage. He held out a $20 bill. She leaned down, and he whispered in her ear, "There's more where this came from. And I've got some blow." She responded, "My name is Angel, and this is my last number."

"Meet me in the back in ten minutes. You'll have the time of your life."

The act finished, Morgan left a tip on his table and sauntered to the parking lot. They met in the back corner of the parking lot. Morgan suggested they go in his car and head back to his apartment. "Let me see the stuff, first," Angel said, all business. Morgan took the coke out of his pocket and showed her. "Let's go, boss!" Angel said enthusiastically.

The sex was long and furious. Arms and legs were flailing. "This is great," Morgan thought to himself, "things are finally turning around." They did it every which way for what seemed like hours. Finally, they both drifted off.

Morgan did not stir until a few rays of light found their way through the vertical blinds. He looked over, but she was gone! He rummaged around to find his pants. He put them on, but there was something missing. She had lifted his wallet.

7

Over the next several days, Gideon did nothing much else but go through the documents. As he noticed things of interest, he put colored paperclips on the document so that he could review them again later. Nothing really jumped out at him. The personnel file was pretty standard. It contained Morgan's resume, an employment application for Western Health Corp., a number of performance evaluations, various payroll documents, attendance cards and health insurance election forms. Just as Greene and Morgan's supervisor, Ben Williams, had said, Morgan had been warned a number of times about his lack of productivity and his tardiness.

The final warning issued to Morgan two months before he was fired explicitly said that if he was tardy or absent without adequate explanation, or if he did not bring his productivity up to the levels he had reached the past couple of years, he would be terminated from employment. There was further documentation showing that in the two months after the written warning, Morgan had been absent six days for no reason whatsoever and had been tardy on a dozen other occasions. When Williams asked Morgan for his doctor's verification of his absence, Morgan flatly refused to provide it. Williams recommended to Greene that Morgan be terminated, but

Greene decided to have a final meeting with Morgan to see if they could rectify the situation.

Greene took notes of the meeting, which were in Morgan's personnel file. The notes reflected that Greene had asked Morgan to agree to weekly production goals that would eventually bring his marketing production up to the point that it had been about a year ago. Morgan refused, saying that no other employee had to do that, so why should he? Greene also asked Morgan whether the company could do anything to help him with his tardiness and absence problems. He specifically asked Morgan whether he was having any personal problems with which the company could assist him.

Morgan said he had no personal problems, and that Greene should mind his own business. Greene then advised Morgan that he felt he had no alternative but to terminate him, and told him that he would be willing to prepare a letter of recommendation and provide any outplacement assistance he needed in finding a new job. At that point, according to Greene's notes, Morgan left the room and slammed the door behind him.

Gideon knew that Morgan would have an explanation for his tardiness and his lack of productivity, but it certainly didn't seem to come through from the personnel file. The one thing Gideon thought might explain the tardiness and bizarre behavior was some sort of alcohol or drug problem. He would ask the usual questions in the deposition, but was relatively certain he would get the usual denials. If only he had something else to go on, he might try to do some investigation to find out whether Morgan indeed had any such difficulties. Nothing, however, in the personnel file gave him any leads.

Gideon went through the remainder of the documents during that week. The personnel policies and benefit information were of little value. Western Health Corp.'s personnel policies were fairly standard. They specifically permitted termination of employment for such misconduct as tardiness and excessive absenteeism, as well as lack of productivity. Western Health Corp. had a system called progressive discipline, whereby the employee would generally be warned for the first offense of these work rules, but could be terminated after any such warning.

The whole issue in this case would be whether Western Health Corp. could prove that it had good cause to terminate Morgan from employment. Morgan, of course, would claim that Western Health Corp. terminated him for an illegal reason – complaining about the safety of Western Health Corp.'s signature drug, Marvil.

One of the things that Gideon knew he would have to do if the case went to trial was to convince the jury that Marvil was in fact safe, and did not cause any health problems that Morgan would claim it did. He knew that he would have to become completely conversant with the scientific testing documents that were presented before the FDA. He went through these documents in meticulous fashion. Whenever he had any question about terminology, he wrote himself notes and a list of questions to ask Alex Benczik, the chief chemist. He even took out some books from the library on medicine

41

to assist him in understanding the various tests performed.

Although Gideon didn't understand all the terminology in the documents, one thing came through perfectly clear. Marvil had been subjected to rigorous testing; there was comprehensive data regarding its test results on laboratory animals and on humans; and all the tests showed there were no adverse effects, short or long term, from the drug, Marvil. Indeed, the tests showed that the drug did not even cause drowsiness, nausea, or lack of sexual drive – all common side effects of other antidepressant drugs.

One of the boxes of documents was entirely comprised of the notes of the chief chemist, Alex Benczik. Benczik had been personally involved in the testing of Marvil from its creation all the way through FDA approval. There were nearly three years of daily notes and logs kept by Benczik. Gideon went through these page-by-page. It took him nearly two days to go through the entire box of notes. When he had finished, Gideon could only draw one conclusion: Even with mega doses given to laboratory animals, Marvil had not shown any signs of causing any disease or other abnormal side effects.

In fact, Benczik's notes were filled with entries showing Benczik's own surprise with the results. Thus, Benczik noted at one that point that, "No drowsiness or lack of motor function shown in animals with 20 milligram dose – remarkable." An entry the day later compared the rat's reaction on the prior day with a 20-milligram dose of Valium: "Subject animal exhibits disorientation and sluggish movement within thirty minutes of dosage – returns to

42

normal pace six hours later." Similar entries appeared throughout the lengthy notes of Alex Benczik.

It took Gideon the remainder of the week to get through the documents. On Friday afternoon, he spoke with McCabe about his findings. McCabe and Gideon agreed that they ought to now go ahead and answer the Complaint and immediately set the deposition of Morgan. Gideon and McCabe called Greene jointly and advised him of their game plans. Greene was pleased.

"I hope those documents give you some indication of the care we took in the marketing of Marvil," Greene said. "We did not submit Marvil to the FDA until we were completely sure that it was safe, and it was not marketed until we received a ringing endorsement from the FDA." Gideon told Greene that he was indeed impressed by the thoroughness of Benczik's notes and the testing procedures. McCabe and Gideon ended the conversation by assuring Greene that an answer would be filed at the beginning of the following week and that the deposition would take place 15 days thereafter.

After they completed the conversation, McCabe and Gideon spoke briefly in the office. "Get that Answer prepared, and let's get it on filed on Monday," McCabe said to Gideon. "I don't need to see it before it's filed, let's just get it done." Before Gideon could respond, McCabe's phone rang, and he was waved out of the room.

Preparing the Answer was not a difficult task. Gideon had done literally dozens of them before; indeed, the labor department had a form in the computer which only needed to be modified slightly. An Answer can simply deny generally all of the allegations in the plaintiff's Complaint, without going into any great specifics. Then, the defendant typically sets forth a number of legal defenses which, it claims, requires judgment in its favor. Only a few of the defenses ever come into play. The remainder are put in simply out of an over-abundance of caution, in case some new facts present itself or some legal defense which is not currently recognized becomes important at a later date. Gideon put the necessary modifications in the Answer, and had his secretary run it through. He would have no trouble getting it filed by Monday.

Gideon was happy that he would not have to work over the weekend. He and Ali planned to spend a quiet weekend together, perhaps going to dinner and a movie, and finally getting to the house projects Gideon had promised to help on earlier in the week. He did, however, pack the personnel file in his document bag prior to leaving the office. If he had a few minutes, he would review it again and perhaps come up with some witness or leads into Morgan's erratic behavior.

The weekend was extremely pleasant. Both Gideon and Ali actually had the whole weekend off together.

Although many lawyers made it a practice to go into the office one or both days over the weekend, Gideon tried to do so only in the worst of emergencies. He would frequently take work home with him and do a few hours here and there when he wasn't doing anything else. He hated, however, to go to the office on the weekend. Not only did it break the day, but he simply found it terribly depressing being in downtown Los Angeles over the weekend.

Unlike the week, when the streets are packed with lawyers and businessmen, downtown Los Angeles is a virtual wasteland over the weekend. Except for a few homeless people, literally no one is on the streets. Even worse, the office itself is not air conditioned over the weekend and it is uncomfortable to work even for a couple of hours. Few partners show up at the firm over the weekend, but most of the associates do. Gideon had the impression that associates did so because they felt that partners would somehow know that they were in the office over the weekend even when they were not there. Gideon was a year away from being considered for partner.

Partnership had its allure. The average salary for partners at Longworth & Drucker was about $800,000.

Beginning partners made over $500,000. It had its downsides, though. Partners were expected to sacrifice everything for work. Even some partners who had been with the firm 20 years were being asked to relocate to New York and other office locations. Some were put on cases which required them to spend years in Texas, New Mexico, Alaska and other states. None of this appealed to Gideon.

Even more importantly, Gideon had serious doubts whether he wanted to spend his life defending huge companies in the corporate law firm culture. He had vowed to stay at Longworth & Drucker for two years tops to get the best legal training; it had now been nearly six years. He was not sure why he had stayed. While he liked the work generally, he was put off by the conservatism, particularly in the labor department. Strikers were greedy. Fired employees were liars. Discrimination claims were frivolous. This was the lore in the department.

Gideon longed to work on the other side. He wanted to represent individuals who were fired or who were claiming discrimination. While some law firms in town represented both management and employees, Longworth & Drucker's policy strictly forbade it.

Gideon had not decided whether he would stay. He did, however, avoid the "work every day" syndrome. Gideon never really understood that mindset. He would much prefer to work a few extra hours each day during the week and have the weekends, than to waste time downtown with the hope that someone would notice. He hoped that the bottom line was quality of work done and productivity, not whether someone came to the office very weekend and billed tons of hours. Sometimes, unfortunately, he wasn't sure.

Ali, too, had to work frequently on the weekends. An interior designer's clients usually work during the week and it's only on the weekends that they are available for consultation. Frequently, this meant that Ali spent the majority of her Saturday with various clients. However, rarely would she spend much time on a Sunday, but occasionally it meant taking an hour or two. On Saturdays, when Ali was working, Gideon filled his time playing basketball and working around the house. He also used the time to get any legal work he needed to get done. All in all, it worked out pretty well, even though they did not spend quite the as much time together as both had hoped.

Gideon did not even open up his document bag the entire weekend. Finally, on Sunday night, while Ali was watching a movie on TV, Gideon decided to look through the personnel file a second time. He found nothing of great interest until he reviewed the employment application again.

Western Health Corp. had a standard employment application, which asked the employee to answer a number of questions: "List each and every job you have held since graduating college." Morgan's job history itself was not especially revealing. Prior to going into the marketing and sales department at Western Health Corp., Morgan had held only two other jobs.

After graduating college from U.S.C. in 1983, Morgan had worked for a small computer company for one year as a computer salesman. Apparently, the computer company that he worked for went bankrupt. He then worked until the beginning of 1986 as a stockbroker for a reputable brokerage house. According to the employment application, he left that position because he did not find the work interesting. He began the Western Health Corp. job in 1987 and worked there until his termination in 1993.

None of this seemed at all unusual, except for one thing: Gideon noticed this time around that Morgan had not worked for over a year between the time he left the brokerage house and the time he started at Western Health Corp. Perhaps there was some explanation for the gap of employment that would prove helpful in the case.

8

The weekend was not as kind to Jacobs. He spent most of it in his office trying to come up with an angle for the case. He knew he could rely on Morgan's testimony, but he needed something more concrete. He had to find some direct link between Morgan's termination and his concerns about the safety of Marvil.

Jacobs was about to pack it in for the night. He was not feeling good about the case. He knew it would be difficult trying to bring this case against Western Health Corp. and its big firm lawyers. It was about midnight when Jacobs turned out the light and started to head out of the office. He had gotten two steps in the hallway when the phone rang. Must be a crank call, Jacobs thought. The phone kept ringing. Jacobs turned around and headed back to the office to pick it up.

"Hello. Is this Bill Jacobs?" the voice on the other end asked.

"Yes, it is, who is this?"

"I can't tell you that Mr. Jacobs. But I'm calling about this Western Health Corp. case that you are currently litigating. You are representing Jerry Morgan, aren't you?"

"Yes, I am. Who is this?"

"I'm simply not in a position to tell you, Mr. Jacobs. But I think I have some information that is useful for you."

"Are you interested?"

Of course, Jacobs was interested. He had very little to go on at this point. He wondered who this caller was, and whether it was a set up. He decided to roll the dice.

"I am very interested. What type of information do you have?"

"Your client, Jerry Morgan, was on to something. I can't go into the details now."

"Just tell me this," Jacobs asked. "Are you an employee of Western Health Corp.?"

"I'm not in a position to reveal that either at this time. I just wanted to make contact with you. I will be calling you again about this case. But I just wanted to let you know, don't give up the ship. Your guy Jerry Morgan was on to something."

The phone clicked.

Jacobs was completely confused. Who could this caller be? And why Sunday at midnight? He thought it might simply be a pack of lies. But something in him made him feel that the caller was sincere. There was tension in the voice on the other end. Fear was in the air.

9

Gideon had jotted down the name of Morgan's supervisor at the stockbrokerage company, and called him first thing on Monday to find out if he knew what Morgan did with his year off before his employment with Western Health Corp. The supervisor was friendly but of little help. He said that Morgan had been unhappy from the day he began his job as a stockbroker, and in his view, it was only a matter of time until Morgan left and did something else. Near the end of his employment at the stockbrokerage firm, Morgan was absent on occasion but nothing excessive. In fact, the supervisor said that he had so informed Ben Williams of Western Health Corp., when Williams was checking Morgan's references. All in all, Morgan was an adequate performer, but simply not all that interested in being a stockbroker. This seemed to square with what Morgan had written on the employment application. Normally Gideon would have just let the issue drop at this point and would have questioned the witness in the deposition. However, for some reason, he felt there was something fishy here. Both Western Health Corp. and the stockbrokerage house mentioned that Morgan on occasion displayed some bizarre behavior and had been tardy or absent from employment. Gideon knew it was a long shot, but he thought perhaps it would be worthwhile to get a private investigator to try to reconstruct what Gideon had done in the year of 1986. He decided to go down to McCabe's office to raise the issue with him prior to doing anything further.

McCabe was receptive to the idea. "Why don't you call Greene and tell him what your thoughts are and get his approval. I'll bet that Ted will think that's a good idea and tell you to go ahead. It may lead to nothing, but then again, maybe we'll find out something important here."

Gideon went back to the task of preparing for Morgan's deposition. Taking a plaintiff's deposition may well be the most important thing a lawyer does during the course of litigation. Although one purpose of a deposition is to simply find out all the facts the plaintiff has to support his claims, there is much more to it.

A good lawyer can trap even the savviest witness, if he prepares for and plans his deposition questions correctly. It's crucial before taking a deposition to know precisely what the legal requirements are for a given case and to try to get admissions from the plaintiff which will make it impossible for him to pursue the case. This is because, in most cases, a defendant will try to bring a motion before trial to dismiss the case. These motions are only successful if there are major admissions in the plaintiff's testimony.

In this case, Gideon knew that it would be difficult to get a dismissal before trial. His only hope, thus far, was to show that Morgan knew nothing about chemistry or the testing of drugs for

FDA approval and could not possibly have known if a product was unsafe. He also wanted to nail Morgan down on the issue of whether he told anyone prior to being fired about his suspicions regarding Marvil. If he could get good admissions as to these two issues, he might have a chance of arguing in a motion to dismiss that Western Health Corp. had good cause to discharge Morgan based on his absenteeism and bizarre workplace behavior.

Morgan would argue that this was not the real reason Western Health Corp. fired him, but rather it did so in retaliation for his reporting concerns about Marvil. Thus, it was crucial to show that no one at Western Health Corp. knew of Morgan's concerns and that the product was in fact completely safe. If he could get these admissions through deposition testimony, Western Health Corp. might well avoid the time and expense of going to trial.

Gideon drafted a number of questions in these two areas. He would go to a deposition with a lengthy outline, but never would follow it word for word. The best depositions are those where the plaintiff volunteers some information that is not directly related to a particular question, and through good follow up questions, the plaintiff makes an important admission. He would not know how good a witness Morgan was, of course, until he took the deposition.

Gideon worked solidly the remainder of the week preparing for the deposition. Through his document review, he was able to ascertain that Morgan had no scientific background, and thus decided to focus on that issue right in the beginning of the deposition to put Morgan on the defensive. Often if points are scored early in a deposition and the witness is put on the defensive, the rest of the deposition goes quite well.

Rather than spending a whole lot of time on background information, Gideon decided to go right at Morgan at the beginning of the deposition. While there is some risk involved in such a decision, Gideon felt that this type of case required such tactics. He then would get some more general background information and finish up by finding out what Morgan told to whom and when about his suspicions regarding Marvil.

By Friday, Gideon has not heard at all from the private investigator. He called the investigator early Friday afternoon. The investigator's report was not promising. "We really haven't come up with much yet, Gideon. We've been able to trace all of Morgan's prior addresses. He has lived in the same apartment since 1987. From 1983 until early 1986, when he left the brokerage firm, he lived in another apartment. We have been able to determine that he stopped his mail at that address about a month after he was fired. The mail was forwarded to his parents who live in Beverly Hills. We suspect that Morgan may have been elsewhere, and that his parents simply collected his mail for him while he was away. Unfortunately, we just can't figure out where he was."

Gideon took this information in stride. Nine times out of ten, such investigations turn up little useful information.

It is the one out of ten that makes it all worthwhile. "Is there anything else you can do to try to find out about Morgan's where-abouts?" Gideon asked. "Money is no issue, here, so don't worry about it."

The investigator hesitated. "There is possibly one more thing we could do. It's a remote possibility, but worth a chance, I guess. Morgan's prior apartment manager mentioned something about Morgan leaving suddenly without giving notice, and his parents having to pay the last month's rent and move his furniture out. Although he doesn't seem like the type of guy, maybe he fell into some problem with the law and got arrested. We could check the police records at the various courthouses for 1986. It's going to take time, and it's going to cost."

Gideon thought about it for a minute. It seemed like quite a long shot, but then again, Greene had given him the go-ahead to do whatever was necessary. "See what you folks can find, and do it as quickly as you can. I've got to start his deposition on Monday. It'll probably last about two or three days, but the you can get it to me, the better off we'll be." The investigator assured Gideon that he would begin the court search that afternoon and go full guns with a number of the various courts on Monday.

Gideon decided to give Ted Greene a full rundown of the investigator's report before the weekend. He had a good conversa-tion with Greene. Greene was completely in favor of going the extra yard to try to find out more information about Morgan. Greene also told Gideon that rather than sending Ben Williams, Morgan's immediate supervisor, to sit in on the deposition, he would send Alex Benczik. Gideon thought this was a good idea. It seemed more and more the focus of this case would be on the safety of the drug Marvil and not so much on Morgan's performance problems. It was in the area of testing Marvil that he would need Benczik's scientific expertise.

Gideon asked Greene to have Benczik arrive about a half hour before the deposition was scheduled to begin the following Monday. Gideon wanted the opportunity to go over some of the Marvil testing procedures, so that he could ask questions about them to Morgan during the deposition. Greene said that he would advise Benczik to arrive no later than 9:00 a.m. on Monday.

After his conversation with Greene, Gideon did some final preparation for the deposition. He took home his deposition outline, as well as some of the documents he planned to use as exhibits at the deposition. He planned to review them on Sunday evening to brush up for the deposition.

The weekend proved to be relaxing and pleasant. Gideon and Ali got to spend some time together and to complete the project they had begun around the house. They went out to dinner both Friday and Saturday night with friends and took in a movie late Sunday afternoon. It was not until about 9:00 p.m. on Sunday that Gideon reviewed his deposition outline and the exhibits for the Morgan deposition.

Gideon read through the exhibits one more time carefully,

hoping that something would jump out at him. Nothing struck him until he read through once again the standard questions contained on the employment application. One of the questions was, "Have you ever served in the military?" Again, Morgan checked the box "no" to that question.

The next question was, "Do you have any physical condition that would prevent you from performing your job?" Again, Morgan checked the box "no" next to the question.

The final question was one that often appeared on employment applications. It asked, "Have you ever been convicted of a felony?" Although Gideon had read over the employment application on several occasions, he now noticed for the first time that no box had been checked next to that question. While this may have been just an oversight on the part of Morgan, Gideon wanted to make sure. He decided to call the private investigator first thing in the morning and tell him to expand his search of the criminal records beyond 1986 to any time in the past.

Gideon arrived early to work the next morning. He immediately called the private investigator, and told him to search the criminal records for the 1970's as well as the 1980's. Perhaps Morgan had gotten into some trouble in high school or shortly thereafter, and it might help explain where he had been in 1986.

Benczik arrived about ten minutes before nine. He and Gideon chatted about the case over a cup of coffee, and Gideon explained to Benczik what would occur in the deposition. Gideon asked Benczik to bring a pen and pad into the deposition and to take notes during the deposition with respect to any issue that Benczik felt was not adequately covered, or which Morgan was wrong about. Gideon told Benczik that during the breaks in the deposition, they could discuss those issues and that Gideon would cover them during the next session. He advised Benczik not to say anything during the deposition or to speak with Morgan during the breaks, other than to say hello or to make idle conversation. Gideon particularly did not want Benczik to tell Morgan anything about what was going on at the company or the company's reaction to the lawsuit.

At about 9:20 a.m., the court reporter arrived for the deposition. On a stenotype shorthand machine, the court reporter transcribes all of the questions and answers during the deposition. After the deposition is completed, she will convert this recording of the day's events into a transcript. The average length of a deposition for a day's questions and answers is about 200 pages. Gideon expected that this type of case would take two to three days to go through the documents and to ask all the necessary questions.

By 9:45 a.m., neither Morgan nor his counsel had arrived for the deposition. This was pretty much part for the course, but it nonetheless frustrated Gideon every time it happened. He simply couldn't understand why people were always late to their depositions. Usually, they started from a half hour to an hour late, and then the person being deposed asked for frequent breaks. Naturally, when this occurred, the deposition did not proceed as quickly as their side had hoped, and that meant additional days of deposition were necessary. Gideon always felt that if he was able to begin a deposition on time and proceed with a minimum of breaks and objections from the other counsel, he could complete any deposition in these type of cases in a day or a day and a half.

At 10:00 a.m., Gideon's phone rang. It was the reception announcing that Morgan and his counsel, Bill Jacobs, had arrived. Gideon asked his secretary to go to the reception area and bring the plaintiff and his counsel to the deposition room. Gideon and Benczik proceeded to the deposition room and awaited Morgan and his counsel. They arrived about a minute later, and the exchange was pleasant. Morgan shook both Gideon's hand and Benczik's and extended his regards to Benczik. Jacobs asked Gideon to step in the hallway for a minute so they could talk about the deposition.

Benczik and Morgan seated themselves in the deposition room, and Gideon and Jacobs walked down the hallway. "How long do you think this will last?" Jacobs asked Gideon. "I really can't say," Gideon replied. "I plan to move quickly, but there are a lot of documents and I need to get all the facts from Morgan. If we can minimize the breaks and start tomorrow on time, I would hope to finish then."

Jacobs gave the standard response of opposing counsel. "I really didn't plan for this to go more than one day. I'll have to call my office at a break and find out whether I can swing it for tomorrow. Otherwise we'll have to reschedule it."

"I don't have a problem if you need to reschedule," Gideon replied. "But if we do so, we have to agree on a date certain to continue the deposition and you have to agree not to do any discovery yourself until I complete Mr. Morgan's deposition."

"I'm not prepared to enter into any such agreement," Jacobs shot back. "Then I guess we'll have to go as long as we can today and finish up the deposition tomorrow," Gideon said coolly. "Let's get going on this. It's already 10:15 a.m."

As he walked to the deposition room, Gideon knew that one of two things would happen. Either Jacobs would free up the time to continue the deposition the next day, or he would agree to the postponement with the conditions set by Gideon. He had never once heard an opposing counsel agree to such a discovery schedule from the start, but as the day wore on, they always did. Gideon actually preferred that the deposition be postponed, giving his private investigator some more time to look into Morgan's whereabouts. But he also knew that Greene wanted to move quickly in this case, so he did not want to offer any lengthy postponement.

As Gideon headed back to the deposition room, he caught his secretary out of the corner of his eye waving a message she had taken. He walked past the desk, picked up the message and continued into the room. He did not want to postpone the beginning of the deposition any longer. As the parties sat down to begin the deposition, Gideon unfolded the message paper. It was a message from his private investigator with the word "URGENT" written on it.

10

The Morgan case had put a big strain on Ali. She had been used to Gideon's long hours in the past. But this case had taken on a dynamic of its own. Gideon was possessed with it. He spent every waking hour thinking about his strategy in defending the case. He was consumed.

Even so, Ali had decided that getting angry at Gideon was not the best way to handle the situation.

Rather, she found the whole case very interesting. She decided to do her own research about Marvil.

She was spending every moment of her free time in the local library. She had become conversant with FDA procedure and chemical compounds. She had begun to think that Gideon was a bit naive about the case. From what Gideon told her, Marvil had been approved by the FDA in record time, and then someone thought it was unsafe. Next thing you know, that person was fired. A coincidence, maybe. But Ali wanted to know for sure.

She had heard Gideon talk ad nauseam about Western Health Corp.'s witnesses. Ted Greene was a god. A boy wonder. One of the youngest CEOs in the country. Alex Benczik was the typical mad scientist. Work was everything. A dedicated soldier. Above reproach. Ben Williams was bombastic, but competent. A paper warrior. Very detail oriented.

Ali knew that it would be highly improper for her to meet any of these witnesses. But there was nothing wrong, was there, with her doing a little bit of snooping on her own. Perhaps she could find out something that would help her husband defend this case.

11

"Ms. Court Reporter, would you please swear in the witness?" With those words, Gideon began the deposition.

The court reporter asked Morgan to raise his right hand and to swear to tell the truth. Morgan responded affirmatively.

"Mr. Morgan, have you ever had your deposition taken before?" Gideon began in a confident tone.

"No, I haven't," Morgan answered. Gideon then explained how the deposition would work, much as he had done at dozens of depositions before. Any lawyer taking a deposition wants to make sure that the witness fully understands what is taking place. Typically, the lawyer asking the questions will tell the witness that he must answer all the questions verbally, that the court reporter will take everything down, that she will transcribe the proceeds into a deposition transcript, that he will have a chance to review the transcript and make any necessary changes, but that if any changes were made, he (Gideon) would comment about the changes at the trial.

Gideon reminded Morgan that he had sworn to tell the truth under penalty of perjury, and that the oath taken at the beginning of the deposition was the same oath taken in a court of law. He told

Morgan that if he did not understand any of the questions to say so, and that Gideon would gladly rephrase the question.

After each of these instructions, Gideon asked Morgan if he understood them. Morgan responded, "Yes," each time.

At this point in a deposition, Gideon would typically elicit some background information from the plaintiff, such as the date of birth, education and family background. In this case, however, Gideon jumped right into the meat of the case.

Q: "Your job at Western Health Corp. was marketing the various medications to pharmacies, isn't that right?"

A: "That's correct."

Q: "You don't do any testing of the drugs in the lab, do you?"

A: "No."

Q: "That's what chemists like Mr. Benczik do, isn't that right?"

A: "That's right."

Q: "And you didn't perform any tests on the drug Marvil, did you?"

At this point, Jacobs interrupted the deposition. "I need to confer with my client for a moment. Let's take a five-minute break." Gideon had more ground to cover on this issue and was displeased that the deposition would be interrupted.

"Let me note for the record that opposing counsel has interrupted this deposition right in the middle of my questions and is now conferring with his witness," Gideon stated.

He did this both for the effect and in case Morgan came back to the deposition well coached and began trying to backtrack on his answers. He could always point out that Jacobs had conferred with him at this point in the deposition at the time of trial.

Gideon took the opportunity to head back to his office and call the private investigator. The investigator could hardly contain himself.

"You're not going to believe this, Gideon," the investigator began. "We found absolutely nothing in the police records for 1986, but we went back further. It seems that our friend Mr. Morgan was arrested in the summer of 1979 for using PCP - angel dust. That was the summer between high school and college. It was his first offense, and with his parents' influence, he got probation and a month in a psychiatric ward at the private hospital about 30 miles from here."

"You've done a great job," Gideon told the investigator. "Gideon, wait, there is more," the investigator offered. "When Morgan was arrested, he was sitting on his front lawn stark naked with a shotgun in his hands. He was threatening to kill everyone around him when the officers finally subdued him."

Gideon couldn't believe his ears. "Do you think this guy's dangerous?" Gideon asked. "Gideon, he may be. PCP is one of those drugs which can cause periodic flashbacks and delusions. This may have happened more than once." Gideon got the name of the private hospital that Morgan had been sent to and asked the investigator to hand deliver the police records.

He immediately called McCabe and relayed to him the information. "I think we should get a subpoena out as soon as we can." Gideon told McCabe. McCabe agreed. Gideon told McCabe that he would get a fellow associate to prepare the subpoena while he went back into the deposition room.

"You may get a fight from the opposing counsel about this," McCabe stated. "Let's not advise him that we are sending the subpoena out until the end of the day. Then serve the subpoena on him. You may need to gear up for a court battle on this."

Gideon called an associate who had worked with him on a number of other cases. Allen Henderson had been at the firm for a little over a year and was still learning the ropes. Henderson had worked with Gideon on a new case, and the two had become close. Both had the same liberal political leanings, and Gideon had become a sort of mentor to Henderson. Gideon knew that Henderson would jump right on the project.

Gideon explained to Henderson that he wanted to subpoena all medical records with respect to Jerry Morgan from the years 1979 to the present. "I'll draft up the subpoena and have it ready for you to review at your lunch break," Henderson told Gideon. "If there is anything else you need me to do on this case, just let me know."

Gideon knew that he would not be able to obtain the documents before the next session of Morgan's deposition. He had to give the hospital reasonable time to locate the documents and to produce them. In addition, Morgan could file what is called a motion to quash the subpoena. That is a motion filed in court which asks the judge to refuse to permit the other side to obtain the documents. Morgan's counsel would likely claim that the documents invaded his client's privacy and were not relevant to the lawsuit. Given the inevitable time delay in getting the documents, Gideon decided to revisit the issue of continuing Morgan's deposition with Jacobs.

Gideon went back to the deposition room. Prior to starting the questioning, he asked Jacobs whether he had called his office to find out about his calendar.

"I just can't do this deposition tomorrow," Jacobs said. "I'm really not planning to do much discovery anyhow, so I'll agree to your conditions. The next full free day I have is two weeks from today. I know that's a while, but if I don't do any discovery, I can't see how you would be harmed by the delay."

Normally, Gideon would push for an earlier date. But he felt the extra time would do him good. He would explain the delay to Greene, and he was sure that Greene would not mind. "That's fine." Gideon said. "Let's put that on the record."

The deposition resumed. Gideon put on the record that the parties had agreed to take the next day of Morgan's deposition in two weeks. Gideon then had a strategy decision to make. He could continue with his line of questioning about Morgan's lack of chemistry background and lack of knowledge about the testing procedures with respect to Marvil. Or, he could move on to a completely different subject, and touch on that area later. Given that Gideon was sure that Morgan had been carefully prepared by his counsel during the break, he decided to take a different route.

Armed with his information about Morgan's problems during the summer of 1979, Gideon decided to ask some fairly basic questions about Morgan's background. He might be able to trap Morgan lying about the summer of 1979, which could cost Morgan dearly with a judge or a jury later on. Gideon resumed the deposition with some innocuous questions about Morgan's background. He got Morgan's date of birth, the name of his parents and siblings, and his educational history. Morgan had graduated from high school, as Gideon already knew, in 1979 and had gone to USC the following fall. He graduated USC on time in 1983. Gideon then asked Morgan to give his employment history. Morgan began with 1983, and described the jobs that Gideon already knew about. When Morgan finished, Gideon asked some follow up questions.

"Now, you mentioned employment beginning in 1983, were you employed any time during high school or college?"

Jacobs objected to this question. "What possible relevance does that have, counsel?" This case involves employment at Western Health Corp. I just can't see what the relevance is of these questions."

Gideon wasn't that surprised to receive an objection at this point. Most counsel at some point early in the deposition will make some objections to let his client know that he is there fighting for him. As to this line of questioning, however, there wasn't any merit to the objection.

"Mr. Jacobs, you know as well as I do, that I am entitled to some background information. It may lead to relevant evidence or it may not, but I'm certainly entitled to a little leeway. I am almost finished." Jacobs permitted Morgan to answer the question.

"I held some odd jobs during high school and college. Nothing terribly exciting. I worked in a grocery store, I worked as a lifeguard, and I sold some computer equipment during my last couple years of college."

Gideon wanted to get precise dates from Morgan. "When exactly did you work for the grocery store?"

Morgan said that it was during his sophomore and junior years of high school.

"And when did you work as a lifeguard?" Morgan responded that he worked as a lifeguard during the summers after his freshman and sophomore years at USC. Gideon saw an opening.

"Now you say that you worked the summers after your sophomore and junior years in high school, and after your freshman and sophomore years in college. Did you work after your senior year in high school?"

Gideon looked at Morgan closely to see if there was any indication of uneasiness.

"I needed to have some fun. So, I didn't work."

"What did you do?" Gideon asked.

"Nothing much," Morgan replied. "I just hung out."

Gideon now noticed that Morgan had begun to squirm slightly in his chest. Gideon would have liked to have sprung the police documents on Morgan at this point, which showed that he was arrested. However, he had not yet obtained the documents from the private investigator. He had asked the private investigator not to fax the document, but to hand deliver it because of its sensitive nature. Still, Gideon felt that he could ask questions regarding Morgan's arrest in good faith.

"Sir, you didn't just hang around that summer, did you?" Gideon stared straight into Morgan's eyes when he asked the question.

"What do you mean by that?" Morgan shot back, his voice increasing several decibels.

"I mean, Mr. Morgan, something else happened that summer, didn't it?"

Morgan turned to his counsel and asked him, "Do I have to answer these questions?"

It was obvious to Gideon that Jacobs had no idea about Morgan's past. "Jerry, these questions aren't terribly relevant, but he is entitled to some background."

"But," Morgan said aloud so that court reporter could get it down, "he's getting into something that's very private. It has nothing to do with this case."

Jacobs finally caught on. "We're taking another break," Jacobs said, as he walked out the door with his client.

Benczik, who had been silent throughout the proceedings so far, asked Gideon what was going on. Gideon realized that he had not even had time to advise Benczik of what he had discovered.

"It seems that Morgan got in trouble with the law before he went to college. He was taking some pretty serious drugs, and he got arrested."

Benczik looked a little perplexed. "How is that going to help us in this case?" Benczik asked.

"It may or it may not," Gideon replied. "Morgan is claiming that he suffered emotional distress because of his termination. We can argue that Morgan had some serious emotional problems in the past, as evidenced by his drug use. A jury night be reluctant to award him a lot of money for stress, which he claims he suffered from a termination. We also may have a more direct link. Ben Williams told me that Morgan had acted pretty bizarrely and was late frequently at the time he was fired. It may be that he got involved in drugs again."

"This is all proving to be very interesting," Benczik said, as Morgan and Jacobs walked back into the room.

Before Gideon could resume the deposition, Jacobs exploded. "I've given you a lot of leeway, and I'm going to stop it right now. You're prying into areas that have nothing to do with this case, and I think you're just trying to harass him."

Gideon responded calmly: "I really don't know if he's got anything relevant to say unless he answers. If he did nothing during the summer, I'll move off it, but I think that he did. This is discovery, and I can find out the information subject to any objection you have, and you can raise an objection later at trial."

Jacobs refused to budge. "He's not answering any further questions about the summer of 1979, period."

"Well," Gideon replied. "I'm going to ask him questions, and you can instruct him not to answer if you wish. But if you do, I'm going to get a court order requiring him to respond." "I don't care what you do," Jacob countered, "he's not answering." Gideon knew that further argument was fruitless at this point. He resumed the deposition.

Q: "Sir, you were arrested in the summer of 1979, weren't you?

Mr. Jacobs: "I instruct the witness not to answer."

Q: "I'm going to seek a court order on that, counsel."

Mr. Jacobs: "Go ahead."

Q: "And the reason you were arrested was for possession of PCP, commonly known as angel dust, isn't that right?"

Mr. Jacobs: "I instruct you not to answer."

Q: "I'm going to go to court on this one as well."

Mr. Jacobs: "Fine."

Q: "And when the police arrested you, you were sitting stark naked in front of your house with a shotgun, isn't that correct?"

Mr. Jacobs: "I instruct the witness not to answer."

Q: "I will seek a court order on that one as well."

Gideon decided to leave that area of inquiry. He had asked the three questions which he wanted Morgan to answer. The questions were simple and direct. If Gideon had persisted and asked further questions, his questions may become harassing and he might risk alienating the judge. As it was, Gideon could argue that these three questions were directly relevant to Morgan's claims of emotional distress and may well be relevant to show the basis for Morgan's bizarre behavior at Western Health Corporation. Although it was far from a sure thing, Gideon thought he had the better argument on this issue.

The rest of the deposition went without further interruption. Gideon asked questions in great detail about Morgan's work history. He got the names of all of Morgan's prior supervisors. He learned that Morgan had not been fired from any other job and had moved each time to a position that paid more money. Gideon purposely didn't ask any questions about 1986 because he didn't have anything to go on at this point. He knew he would simply be greeted with evasive responses and perhaps instructions not to answer.

By 4:00 p.m., Gideon had already asked a number of questions about Morgan's employment at Western Health Corp. He learned how Morgan found out about the job and went through the interview process. He marked as exhibits a number of documents, including his performance evaluations and a letter offering him employment. Again, Gideon purposely did not make anything out of Morgan's failure to check the box on the employment application

73

with respect to whether he had been convicted of a felony. He would go into that after he got the court order requiring Morgan to answer the other questions.

Gideon had also already gone through Morgan's performance reviews for the two years prior to his termination. He was now going to get into the time period in which Morgan's productivity had declined and when Morgan's absenteeism escalated. This was a good time to break for the day, and Gideon suggested to Jacobs that the two conclude the deposition for the moment until the court resolved the issues with respect to the questions that Jacobs had refused to let Morgan answer. He also advised Jacobs that he would be serving a subpoena for medical records on the private hospital north of Los Angeles. Jacobs told Gideon that he would move to quash the subpoena. Gideon suggested that they both file their motions with the court on the same day and argue it all at once. Jacobs agreed.

Prior to completing the deposition, Gideon went out and got the subpoena from Henderson. Gideon had reviewed the subpoena fleetingly during lunch, and it was fine. Henderson had already sent it out to be served on the hospital. Gideon gave the subpoena to Jacobs, and they agreed to file their motions with the court by the end of the week.

Gideon offered to call the judge's clerk to find out what day the judge could hear the motions. Jacobs and Morgan then departed for the day.

It had been a long, but successful day. Gideon felt that he

had made some headway in the deposition, and that he had the upper hand in the lawsuit. Jacobs seemed really worried about the prospect of Gideon getting the evidence about Morgan's drug problems. Gideon knew that he needed to take advantage of this stroke of luck and use it for what it was worth.

He called Ted Greene and advised him of the day's events. Greene was surprised about Morgan's prior drug problem, but was pleased that Gideon had discovered it. Greene suggested that if the court in fact required Morgan to answer the deposition questions and permit Gideon to obtain the documents, they might try to make a low settlement offer to try to end the case while they had the upper hand. Gideon agreed wholeheartedly and promised to do all he could to win the motion in court.

Gideon then went down the hallway to report the day's events to McCabe. McCabe was not in the office, so Gideon left him a long phone message. Right after Gideon left the message for McCabe, his secretary walked in the door with a package. It was the file from the private investigator. Gideon's secretary asked if she needed to stay late. Gideon told her to go home and to expect a lot of typing the next day as Gideon prepared the motion to require Morgan to answer the deposition questions.

Although he was tired, Gideon knew it would be best for him to write a draft of the motion while the events of the day were still fresh. He outlined for the judge the nature of the case and the reasons why the questions were relevant. He had some cases on his side which permitted the discovery of otherwise private information when the person suing was claiming that he suffered emotional distress. Gideon had the additional argument that discovery regarding Morgan's past drug use might be relevant to show why he acted bizarrely during the last six months of work. Gideon asked the judge to require Morgan to answer the three questions, as well as to answer any and all questions about his drug use and/or hospitalizations from 1979 to present. He would attach as an exhibit to the motion the court records which the private investigator had obtained for him. He would need to get the investigator to sign a declaration saying that these were accurate copies of records obtained from the criminal courthouse. He decided to take care of that aspect of the motion in the morning.

Gideon left the office about 8:30 that evening. He knew that the next several weeks would be critical, and that the upcoming court battle could well be a turning point in the case.

12

Ed Miles was a career bureaucrat. He had worked for the government for 34 years. At age 59, he was a year before retirement and a sizeable pension. He never earned a lot of money working for the government, but he would be able to live modestly the rest of his life on his pension.

Miles had been with the FDA for nearly a quarter century. He was a quasi-administrator and a quasi-scientist. He had graduated from Harvard with a degree in chemistry and did his doctoral dissertation there as well. Rather than going into private industry, he had started doing some research in the Defense Department, but jumped at the opportunity to move into the FDA when a position was offered to him several years later. During the early years with the FDA, he was part of the team that would go out and inspect the test results of pharmaceutical companies attempting to gain approval to put their product on the market. In later years, after a number of promotions, he coordinated such efforts from his office in Washington, D.C. He rarely, if ever, had to travel any more, which delighted his wife.

Miles was at his desk reviewing a report done by his field investigators regarding their review of a drug which was supposed to stop male pattern baldness. Miles had more than a fleeting interest in the subject; he had been balding for years. That was one of the few perks of the job. If, in fact, a drug was approved, he could expect to receive a lifetime supply of it. Naturally, there was very little that he could or would use. A drug that would stop male pattern baldness, however, was one which he might.

Miles was about to go out to lunch when the day's mail arrived. Most of it was government issue; he noticed one envelope with an address and name on it that he did not recognize. He opened up the envelope and read the two-paragraph letter.

"I represent Jerry Morgan, a former employee of Western Health Corp. in California. Mr. Morgan was terminated from Western Health Corp. last year. I understand that you coordinated the review of Western Health Corp.'s drug Marvil which was approved by the FDA about a year and one half ago."

"I would greatly appreciate the opportunity to talk with you at your convenience regarding Marvil and the FDA approval of it. Please be assured that I do not have any doubts about the thoroughness of the FDA's review of Marvil; I simply would like to gather as much information as I can about the process. If I do not hear from you shortly, I will call to see if we can arrange a time to talk. Sincerely, Bill Jacobs"

Miles remembered the FDA review of Marvil quite clearly. It was one of the more high-profile matters that the FDA had worked on in the last number of years. He recalled that Western Health

Corp.'s records were in impeccable shape, and with Western Health Corp.'s virtually around-the-clock assistance, the approval process had occurred much more rapidly than usual. He had worked closely with Western Health Corp.'s president, Ted Greene, who had done everything the FDA had asked during the review. He also remembered the thoroughness of the scientist at Western Health Corp. who had assisted Greene, although he could not recall offhand what that fellow's name was.

Still, Miles felt there was nothing wrong in answering any questions Jacobs might have about the approval procedure. He had not heard that any employee of Western Health Corp. had been fired and knew of no reason why any employee's termination would be related to Marvil. He did, however, find Jacob's letter intriguing. He promised himself that he would review the Marvil file before being contacted by Jacobs.

13

Because of the judge's busy calendar, the motions were not scheduled to be heard until about a month after the deposition. Gideon spent most of that time catching up on other cases and took a long weekend with Ali to her parents' house at the beach. He began formal preparation for the hearing about a week before it was scheduled.

Greene was going to attend, as was McCabe. Gideon knew that he would have to be at his best during the argument.

The judge assigned to hear the motion would be the same judge throughout the case. Judge Farmer had been on the Superior Court bench for about a dozen years. He had the reputation of running a tight court room, and he was well regarded as an intellect. He read all the papers filed by the parties and did his own independent research on the cases. If the law was completely on your side, you could be confident of winning. However, if there were any flaws in your case, Judge Farmer would know about them and ask about them during the hearing. He was a good judge for Western Health Corp. in this case, especially because they would make a motion at a later date to try to dismiss the entire case before trial. Gideon thought that this would be a good first opportunity to educate the judge about the case and hopefully to obtain an initial victory.

The hearing was scheduled for 1:30 p.m. Gideon, Greene and McCabe arrived at the courthouse a little after one o'clock. Jacobs arrived shortly thereafter. Morgan did not come to the hearing.

Jacobs sat at the far end of the courtroom and did not even make eye contact with Gideon. Gideon, Greene and McCabe sat together and chatted until Judge Farmer took the bench at exactly 1:30 p.m. They were the only lawyers in the courtroom.

"Case No. 397742," Judge Farmer bellowed. "Morgan v. Western Health Corp. Counsel, would you approach the podium and state your appearances."

Jacobs got to the podium first. "Bill Jacobs, Your Honor, for the plaintiff."

"Good afternoon, Your Honor, Gideon Brown for the defend-ant."

"Gentlemen," Judge Farmer said, "I have read all of your papers. I'd like to hear briefly from both of you. Mr. Brown, why don't you start on your motion regarding the deposition questions."

Gideon gathered his thoughts and made a brief argument to the judge. "Your Honor, the plaintiff in this case is claiming that he suffered severe emotional distress as a result of his termination. During the course of my fact investigation, I learned that Mr. Morgan had been arrested for drug use. I need to inquire into that and get some answers from Mr. Morgan about his drug use. I may well be able to establish that Mr. Morgan had been suffering

81

from emotional distress well before termination from employment, and the jury ought to be able to know this information so that it can determine whether any of Mr. Morgan's alleged emotional distress is attributable to his termination."

"Mr. Jacobs," Judge Farmer declared, "how do you respond to that?"

Jacobs' response was passionate, but not persuasive. "This is all just a ploy, your honor, to harass my client. This case is about Mr. Morgan's unfortunate termination from employment because he suspected that this company's drug was unsafe. It has nothing to do with any trouble Mr. Morgan might have gotten himself into after high school."

"They're just trying to beat up on my client."

"Mr. Jacobs, there's more to it than harassment," Judge Farmer responded. "Your client is claiming emotional distress, and I can see how a jury might find it quite relevant to consider whether there were other factors in Mr. Morgan's life that caused him emotional distress. How else are they to determine how much emotional distress your client suffered from the termination and what they should award him?"

"Judge, I'm not going to have this witness testify that his termination caused him such severe emotional distress that he couldn't function. He's just going to testify that he was very upset about his termination, especially in view of his concerns about the safety of Marvil. The jury knows how it feels to be terminated and will award him emotional distress accordingly."

"That's not going to do it, Mr. Jacobs," Judge Farmer answered. "I can't let your client testify that he was upset about the termination, yet prevent the other side from inquiring how upset he was and whether he was upset about anything else. It seems to me that if you open the door on that issue, they're entitled to go into it."

"Can't we stipulate," Jacobs offered, "that sure, Mr. Morgan was upset about other things in his life, but that he was also upset about his termination? Then let the jury decide how much they want to award him for the distress for his termination."

On several occasions, Gideon wanted to jump in and respond to Mr. Jacobs' arguments. He knew, however, from the judge's questions that the argument was going his way. The hardest thing for a lawyer is to know when to speak and when to be quiet. In this circumstance, Gideon decided that being quiet was the best thing he could do.

"I just can't do that, Mr. Jacobs," Judge Farmer said. "I can't make Mr. Brown stipulate to anything if he doesn't want to. If you open up that door, he's entitled to inquire about other sources of emotional distress. I'm ordering your client, Mr. Jacobs, to appear at his deposition at a date mutually convenient to both you and Mr. Brown. He is to answer all questions about his prior drug use as well as any ramifications from that drug use. Do I make myself clear?"

"Yes, Your Honor," Jacobs stated.

"Now, with respect to your motion, Mr. Jacobs, regarding the medical records of Mr. Morgan. I don't see how the issues there are any different than what I just ruled. I will, however, only permit Mr. Brown to review the documents under a strict order of confidentiality. Mr. Brown, you are not to use those documents for any purpose other than this litigation. The documents are to remain under lock and key in your office at all times. You may use them for exhibits in this case, and after this case is over, you are to return them to Mr. Jacobs and are not to keep any copies. Do you understand that, Mr. Brown?"

"I do, Your Honor, and I will make sure that these documents remain completely confidential."

"All right then, counsel, you have my rulings. I don't want to see you folks in court on any more discovery battles. Take your depositions, produce the documents and let's move along with this case. I expect I'll see you at some point before trial on any pretrial motions either of you may bring. Good day."

The hearing had gone better than even Gideon had expected. He had thought that the judge might limit his questioning in some respect. Judge Farmer, however, had bought the argument: If Morgan was to testify about emotional distress, he was going to allow Gideon to inquire about other sources of it. This would prove to be extremely damaging to Morgan before a jury.

Greene was smiling ear-to-ear as he, McCabe and Gideon walked back to the office from the courtroom. "You did a good job in there, Gideon, you focused the judge on the issue. I'm really pleased the way this case is going so far."

McCabe cautioned Greene that there was a long way to go, that this was just a small victory in a case that might have a lot of hurdles. Still, McCabe shared Greene's enthusiasm with how the case was going. "Gideon, let's get those medical records as quickly as possible. There may be a bombshell there that we don't even know about." Gideon assured McCabe that he would serve a copy of the court's order on the hospital and that they would have the documents within the next couple of days.

The three stopped at a downtown bar for a drink before returning to the office. The case had been active for only about six weeks, but already a lot had happened. By discovering Morgan's hidden past, Gideon was immediately able to shift from being on the defensive to being on the offensive in the case. The more he focused the case on Morgan's past, the better off for Western Health Corp. The three shot the breeze about the Dodgers' playoff chances and ordered another round of drinks. Gideon thought to himself that he might as well enjoy the moment: there were surely many more obstacles to overcome for Western Health Corp. to win the case.

14

The mood in the bar across the street from Jacobs' office was far from jubilant. Jacobs was hopeful that the judge would put some limitations on this line of inquiry and protect his client from disclosing his troubled past. Jack Morgan was downright serious. He did not want his son's past to be disclosed in a public trial which would no doubt receive a lot of press.

"We have got to go on the offensive on this, Bill," Jack Morgan stated. "They're trying to bully us around and doing a good job of it. Isn't there any dirt that we can uncover about Western Health Corp. officials? I mean, if they want to sling mud, let's sling some back."

Jacobs, unfortunately, did not have a lot to offer. "Jack, I've been thinking night and day about this case. I have reviewed all the documents that Jerry gave me, but there's just nothing that I can find to implicate any of these folks. Jerry's testimony about that incident at work will be helpful, but I don't know that it will carry the day. I'm in the process of trying to arrange a meeting with the fellow from the FDA who coordinated the Marvil review procedure. We can only hope that it leads to something."

Jerry Morgan was completely silent during this conversation. He was losing his stomach for the case. He had enough trouble trying to keep his life together, and he did not feel like reliving these difficult times in his past. It was enough that good old Jack would remind him all about it and what a favor he had done for him back in those days.

"Jerry, can you think of anything else that might be useful to us?" Jacobs asked. "Is there anyone at Western Health Corp. who might be helpful to you? The reason I ask is, not that long ago, I got a strange phone call at midnight on a Sunday evening. I did not recognize the voice, and I don't know if it was a Western Health Corp. employee or not."

"All the person said was that you were onto something, and he would call back later in the case. I haven't heard back yet."

Jerry Morgan had little to offer Jacobs. "Bill, I just can't think of anyone who is going to want to step forward from Western Health Corp. Ted Greene has everyone eating out of his hand. He pays these folks an awful lot of money, because the business is incredibly profitable. No one there is going to want to cross him."

"What a goddamn case," Jacobs thought to himself. He needed a break, and he needed one soon.

15

The feverish pace of the case subsided somewhat after the victory in court regarding the hospital records. The hospital had indicated that the records would take about a week to retrieve. Gideon and Jacobs had agreed that the deposition would proceed the week following the hospital's production of the files. That would give both sides a chance to review the documents and prepare for the deposition.

Gideon spent the week catching up on his other cases. He went out to visit Bill Stevens that Wednesday to take him out to lunch and to get up to speed about personnel issues that had arisen at the plant. Although Gideon worked on a number of cases in his five years at the law firm, Stevens was Gideon's only client with whom he dealt on an almost daily basis. Many of his other cases were for large clients who had used the same partner for years. While Gideon would get to know these clients while the case was active, once a case finished, it was the partner who stayed in contact with the client, not the associate. He had been asked, however, to be the point person for Stevens' company, and in the past few years Stevens had grown to rely on Gideon rather than the partner. Stevens would keep the partner up to date, but Gideon pretty much had full run of things with the client.

The remainder of the week was uneventful. Gideon figured he would take a late lunch on Friday and leave early that afternoon to get a head start on the weekend. Late that morning, however, a large package arrived. It was the file from the hospital. Gideon ripped open the package and began looking through the documents. The first several pages were basic medical and family history. He then got to the doctor's report upon Morgan's admission to the hospital after his arrest in 1979. The report confirmed that Morgan was a PCP user: "Subject exhibits behavior typical of long time PCP ingestion. Is currently delusional. Diagnosis: paranoid schizophrenia brought on by PCP ingestion."

Gideon read on. There were numerous doctors' notes and reports chronicling Morgan's progress throughout the summer of 1979. He remained in the hospital until August 1979 – two weeks before he began college at USC. Morgan had ongoing extensive psychiatric counseling for his drug dependency. He had stayed clean throughout the summer and exhibited no more delusional behavior. Upon Morgan's release, his treating physician noted: "Patient ready to interact in society. His progress should be monitored. He may suffer periodic delusions and relapse."

The documents indicated that for the first year after his stay at the hospital in 1979, Morgan was monitored at three-month intervals. However, beginning in the fall of 1980, Morgan apparently stopped coming to the hospital. The medical records indicated a number of phone calls to Morgan's parents requesting that Morgan come in for a checkup. Morgan apparently never did so.

Gideon noticed a stack of documents clipped together underneath the ones he had looked through. He glanced at the top of the first document. It was dated February 23, 1986 – two weeks after he had left his job at the stockbrokerage house. The records indicated that Morgan had been brought to the hospital after being found in an alley. He had ingested a large dose of PCP. The admittance medical report stated that he was delusional and potentially dangerous. He was monitored hourly the first 48 hours in which he was institutionalized. Thereafter, he went into extended counseling. He spent four months in rehab before going to live with his parents. Even after going home, he made weekly visits to the rehab facility to be drug tested. Gideon had a mixed reaction reading this material. On the one hand, he had finally unraveled the puzzle as to Morgan's whereabouts during the year 1986. This information would no doubt help the lawsuit. On the other hand, he felt truly sad for Morgan. Morgan seemed like a nice enough fellow during his deposition, and part of Gideon hated the fact that he would be bringing up Morgan's past when he next deposed him. It would be a tense and unpleasant deposition session.

That evening, Gideon told Ali about what he had discovered about Morgan. Ali felt strongly that Gideon should not bring the issue up unless he could prove that Morgan was on drugs when he was working at Western Health Corp. and that the drug use interfered with his work.

"I just don't see why you get to dig into this guy's entire past simply because he's suing your client," Ali said fervently. "I mean, Gideon, we all have skeletons in our closet, and it's none of our employer's business."

"Yeah," Gideon agreed, "we all do have skeletons. But if you have skeletons, you don't sue your employer for emotional distress. You can sue for your wages and for other damages, but if you sue for emotional distress, you're just opening up your life for inspection. Morgan's lawyer must have told him that, but Morgan went ahead anyhow."

Gideon only half believed what he was saying. He did in fact have reservations about getting into these subjects. The programmed response that he gave to Ali sounded more like an answer to a judge during argument than his honest feelings. Perhaps he had been a lawyer too long.

Gideon had been warned by his law school professors that practicing law would make him more politically conservative. He had seen many of his friends – self-proclaimed liberals – become absolutely reactionary in their quest for the almighty buck. Too often, lawyers became enamored of arguments which, while logical, made no sense when looked at from a moral standpoint. He had begun to tire of pressing arguments for clients that had little chance of succeeding or extracting the last dollar out of a plaintiff's counsel in order to settle a case lower than the client had authorized him to do so. Yet, he was paid handsomely for doing these things for his clients.

Gideon and Ali spoke about the conflict Gideon was facing. Gideon told her that, in a pure moral sense, he felt the same way and did not relish the notion of bringing all of Morgan's past up in the next session of the deposition. He also told Ali that he truly did feel that Western Health Corp. was being sued for no good reason, and that he felt a strong obligation to assist Greene in winning the case in any ethical way possible. He reminded Ali of another case he had worked on in which he really felt his client was in the right, but he had to settle for a large sum because of the sympathy his client and he had felt the jury would feel if the case was tried. Perhaps Morgan's checkered history would be the sort of equalizing factor that would reduce the jury's natural sympathy for a fired employee and lead to a fair and reasonable trial.

That weekend Gideon and Ali took Greene and his wife to a Dodger game. They had dinner before the game at the Stadium Club, which Greene and his wife enjoyed immensely. Gideon himself would have preferred grabbing a couple hot dogs and a beer, but this was a way to spend a little time with Greene to get to know him better. Ali simply hated baseball, but she was a good trooper and had agreed to go along.

The more time Gideon spent with Greene, the more he liked him. Although he was a multimillionaire, he really was a normal guy. He never spoke of his large house or his many cars and never made Gideon feel like he was beneath him. It was clear that he was quite proud of Western Health Corp. and the business he had created. The company's reputation seemed much more important to him than the material items of his private life.

The four watched a close game; the Dodgers coming from behind to win in the bottom of the ninth. Gideon couldn't tell if Ali was more excited by the fact that the Dodgers had won the game or that the game would not go into extra innings. Gideon suspected that it was the latter.

Gideon and Greene bid their goodbyes, and Gideon and Ali began their drive back home. Ali fell asleep in the car in about five minutes. When they arrived home a little over a half hour later, Gideon had to tap Ali on the shoulder, awaken her and lead her into the house. She was asleep in about five seconds flat. Gideon was particularly restless, and his mind raced. He couldn't get over how much Greene loved what he was doing. Gideon wished that he liked his job as much as Greene did his. While Gideon generally enjoyed his day-to-day work, there were times like this that he did not feel fulfilled about being a lawyer. More and more he was dreading the next day of Morgan's deposition. It was going to be war.

16

Jack Morgan was growing ever impatient with Bill Jacobs. While Jacobs was doing his best, he simply wasn't the ball of fire Jack Morgan had hoped would bring Western Health Corp. down to its knees. He was seriously beginning to consider bringing in another lawyer.

Yet, Jack Morgan knew that Jacobs might be on the brink of obtaining some important information. He had, in fact, written a letter to the person who had coordinated the FDA investigation of Marvil. He also had received that anonymous phone call. Perhaps a change in lawyers would undo the few strides that Jacobs had made.

Jack Morgan decided to let this case ride with Jacobs. But Jacobs needed some help. Jack Morgan would not sit idly by. He never in his life sat idly by on anything. He would begin to conduct his own investigation.

Jack Morgan knew that there had to be a soft touch at Western Health Corp. Someone who had an axe to grind with the company. Someone who didn't think that Ted Greene or Western Health Corp. walked on water. The only way to find such an employee was to plant someone there. Jack Morgan knew that

Jacobs would never go for such an arrangement. So, he would take care of it himself.

Jack called one of his old business acquaintances to see if something like this could be set up. The acquaintance led Jack to a private investigation firm who would have an operative apply for employment with Western Health Corp., and hopefully obtain a job quickly. Western Health Corp. happened to have an opening in its mailroom, a perfect position for an operative to assume and have full run of the company.

The operative would go by the name of Jose Gonzales. They doctored up a resume for Gonzales which made him a cinch for the Western Health Corp. position. Western Health Corp., like many major companies, was trying to improve its image with respect to ethnic diversity of its employees. Gonzales would fit the bill. His resume detailed how he had fled from Nicaragua with his family to the United States, and how he was supporting his family through a variety of odd jobs. He was a hard worker, who wanted to learn sales from the bottom up. He would begin working in the mailroom, with the hope of an apprenticeship and someday going into Western Health Corp.'s marketing department. It was the type of rags-to-riches story that the undercover agent knew that Ted Greene and Western Health Corp. would eat up. They would do anything for publicity. Publicity made money.

Gonzales interviewed and was hired for the job. He would prepare reports daily and send them to Jack at the end of each week.

He would meet with Jack each Sunday to strategize and decide what other avenues to pursue. He would also expect Jack to pay him $5,000 each Sunday for his week's endeavor.

17

The next scheduled day of Morgan's deposition finally arrived. This time, Jacobs and Morgan arrived at 9:30 a.m. sharp, and the deposition began on time. Gideon immediately went on attack.

"Q: Now, Mr. Morgan, you will remember that the last time we were here your lawyer advised you not to answer questions about the summer of 1979. Are you aware that the court has ordered you to answer the questions?"

A: "Yes, Sir."

Q: "Mr. Morgan, you were arrested in July 1979, weren't you?"

A: "Yes, that's correct."

Q: "Would you describe the incident, please?"

A: "I really don't remember."

Q: "Nothing at all, Sir?"

A: "No, I tried to wipe it out of my mind. I really don't."

Q: "Let me see if I can refresh your recollection, Sir, the police picked you up in front of your parent's house, isn't that right?"

A: "I believe that is correct."

Q: "You had a shotgun in your hand, isn't that correct?"

A: "I don't remember that."

Q: "Are you saying you didn't have a shotgun in your hand?"

A: "No, that's not what I'm saying. What I'm saying is that I really don't remember."

Gideon saw what was coming. Jacobs had prepared Morgan well this time. A lawyer will typically tell his client who is being deposed not to volunteer any information and that it is perfectly all right to say I don't recall if in fact that is the case. Gideon, however, had seen a lot of witnesses go overboard "following" these instructions. Whenever the questioning got difficult or the topic was something that hurt the witness, the witness suddenly couldn't remember anything. Of course, when it was on a subject that was helpful, the witness had full recollection. This was precisely such a circumstance. Gideon did not think that any judge or jury would possibly believe that Morgan had no recollection whatsoever about his arrest in 1979. He decided to make Morgan look as bad as he could.

Q: "Did you own a shotgun at the time, Mr. Morgan?"

A: "I don't remember."

Q: "Do you have any idea where you got the shotgun?"

A: "I don't even know if I had a shotgun."

Q: "Any reason to believe that this police report is in error?"

A: "No."

Q: "Had you consumed PCP when you were arrested?"

A: "I don't remember."

Q: "Do you know what PCP is?"

A: "Yes."

Q: "You understand that's the same as angel dust?"

A: "Yes."

Q: "You were convicted of a felony, right?"

A: "I don't recall."

Q: "Well if you take a look at this police record, where it says you were convicted of a felony, do you have any reason to believe that is incorrect?"

A: "No, I don't, I just don't remember."

Q: "Then you were institutionalized, right?"

A: "I don't remember."

Q: "Well, you spent time at a private hospital, isn't that right?"

A: "I really don't remember that."

Q: "And you don't have any reason to believe that these medical records from the hospital are incorrect, do you?"

A: "No, I don't, I just don't remember being there."

Jacobs sat silent during this charade. Gideon simply could not imagine what, if anything, Jacobs had up his sleeve. This type of evasive testimony would simply outrage Judge Farmer, Gideon thought to himself. More and more, Gideon was thinking that Morgan's evasive tactics would be quite helpful when he moved to dismiss the case, because it would anger Judge Farmer much more than if Morgan had admitted to the conduct and said he was sorry for it.

Gideon then moved to Morgan's employment application. After asking a few general questions about when Morgan first saw the application and where he filled it out, Gideon focused on the application itself.

Q: "Now, you read this application before you filled it out, isn't that right?"

A: "Yes, I did."

Q: "And you filled out all the information to the best of your knowledge, isn't that right?"

A: "Yes."

Q: "You wouldn't have lied to your prospective employer, right?"

A: "No, of course not."

Q: "I'll turn your attention, Sir, to the question 'were you ever convicted of a felony,' you didn't check yes or no next to that box, did you?"

A: "Now that you mention it, I guess I did not, I guess I just didn't see the question."

Q: "That's the only box on the entire application you didn't fill out, isn't that right, Mr. Morgan?"

Jacobs objected at this point. "Objection, the document speaks for itself, counsel."

Gideon knew that Jacobs' objection was a proper one. "I'll rephrase the question, counsel," Gideon responded. "Mr. Morgan, your employer asked you prior to hiring you whether you had been convicted of a felony, isn't that right?"

Morgan responded "Yes."

"Mr. Morgan, you did not advise your employer one way or the other whether you had been convicted of a felony, isn't that right?" Morgan again responded affirmatively.

The reason Gideon asked those questions was because he knew there was a principle in the law that if an employee falsifies an employment application and the employer later finds out, it might bar the employee from any relief from the employer. Gideon did not have a blatant falsification; it would have been better for his argument if Morgan had checked the box no. He knew that Morgan would go into court with the excuse that he had simply missed the question when signing the employment application. Depending on how the judge viewed Morgan's other testimony, he might or might not believe him.

Gideon then focused Morgan's attention on the 1986 time period.

Q: "You left your job at the stockbrokerage house on February 1, 1986, isn't that right?"

A: "That is correct, Sir."

Q: "One week later you were institutionalized, isn't that right?"

A: "I don't really recall that one way or the other, Sir."

Q: "Do you remember at all what you did during the year of 1986?"

A: "No, I do not."

Q: "You didn't work, did you?"

A: "No, I don't believe I did."

Q: "Had you been ingesting PCP?"

A: "I don't remember."

Q: "Had you been ingesting angel dust?"

A: "I don't remember."

Gideon knew that Morgan would take the same approach as he had done when answering the questions in the 1979 time period. He simply was not going to recall anything about drug use or about being institutionalized. Gideon decided he would not probe into this issue much longer and he simply had the documents from the hospital marked as exhibits to the deposition. He would refer to those when he made his motion to dismiss in court.

The deposition had been going for well over two hours. It was about noon when the parties broke for lunch. Benczik had been quiet during the deposition, and he was no more talkative at lunch. Gideon asked Benczik what he thought about the morning's events.

"He's a strange one," Benczik said, "either he's lying through his teeth or he's totally blacked out these periods. I don't know what to believe."

Gideon was shocked that anyone could even think that Morgan was being anything but a little fast and loose with the truth. "Do you think he really can't remember anything?" Gideon asked.

Benczik backed off his prior statement. "I just wonder if

there's more to this, that's all."

Gideon decided not to discuss the issue with Benczik any further. He had experienced similar types of reactions from company officials sitting in on depositions before. A deposition was generally new to these folks, and they sometimes did not understand the full magnitude of certain deposition admissions because they were not lawyers and had never been in court before a judge or a jury. In addition, many times company officials felt somewhat sorry for the witness. Maybe Benczik felt that Morgan was truly a troubled individual and did not share Greene's sense that Morgan was being vindictive against the company.

The deposition resumed in the afternoon. Gideon went through Morgan's remaining performance reviews and questioned Morgan about the written warnings. Morgan admitted that his production had indeed decreased, but explained it as being cyclical rather than caused by lack of effort. "Like any other business, sometimes our products sell like wildfire and sometimes they don't. It wasn't for lack of effort that I was having trouble moving Marvil and our other products. It was just one of those things," Morgan explained.

Gideon asked Morgan about his absenteeism. "To tell you the truth, things were so slow, I really didn't have much incentive to be in the office. It gets depressing when you're there day after day and no one is buying the product."

"They usually were pretty good about giving us leeway with

our schedules, and I didn't think things would be different this time. I guess I was wrong."

Gideon asked Morgan if he had received the written warning about his absenteeism. Morgan stated that he did. "And you still were absent after you received the warning, isn't that right?" Gideon asked. "Yes, I admit I was absent even after the warning. But, again, I didn't think it was something they would fire me over. I don't think they would have if they didn't think I was on to something."

Gideon had expected that Morgan at some point in the deposition would allude to his suspicions about the safety of Marvil. Gideon decided to waste no time following up.

Q: "Why do you think they felt you were on to something?"

A: "A few things. First of all, I was surprised how fast they were moving along the process of getting Marvil approved by the FDA. It usually takes years after a lab finishes with the chemical to get the FDA in, have them look over all the documents and get approval. Marvil moved at a much faster rate. It couldn't have been more than a year from the time the lab approved it until the FDA gave it the green light."

Q: "Any other reason why you felt Marvil was unsafe?"

A: "Well, one night at about the time the FDA was conducting its review of Marvil, I was walking down the hallway past Ted Greene's office. It was late, about 7:00 p.m. I knew my productivity had been down and I was there late trying to get some marketing leads. Anyhow, I heard two voices in Greene's office. One was Greene; I didn't recognize the other voice. I couldn't hear everything that was going on there, but I did hear Marvil mentioned. All of a sudden, I heard Greene say in a loud voice, 'There's to be no more discussion about this. You know what needs to be done.' I was walking away when Greene opened the door. I did not look back to see who was with Greene, but I'm sure he saw me walking away. Two weeks later I was fired."

Q: "Is there any other reason why you think Marvil is unsafe?"

A: "No, those are the only reasons."

With that admission, Gideon quickly moved on to other subjects and wrapped up the deposition. He had been able to pin Morgan down as to the reasons he suspected Marvil was unsafe. All that Morgan had to go on was the one conversation he overheard in Greene's office, and Morgan's own description of that conversation struck Gideon as not terribly damaging. He felt he would have a strong argument in a motion to dismiss that Morgan's only evidence was a vague comment that may have had nothing to do about the safety of Marvil at all, and that any belief on Morgan's part that Marvil was unsafe was based purely on speculation and conjecture. He would also have the argument to make about Morgan's poor performance and his past institutionalization and drug activity.

Gideon quickly concluded the deposition. He and Jacobs exchanged some pleasantries and said they would agree on dates for the deposition of Western Health Corp.'s officials. Jacobs and Morgan departed, and Gideon and Benczik walked back to Gideon's office to discuss the day's events.

"I should let you know," Benczik began, "that I was the other person in the office the day that Morgan was nosing around Greene's office. Morgan has taken that comment completely out of context. Greene, in fact, during our conversation said, 'There's to be no more discussion about this; you know what needs to be done.' He was referring, however, to my comment to him that the FDA was requiring a ton of information and that I was having trouble getting it all prepared. In essence, he was just telling me to buckle down, to work hard and get everything done. In fact, he promised to send me on a long vacation after the approval process was completed."

"I understand," Gideon replied. "It always amazes me how plaintiffs or their counsel will try to twist an innocent remark and make something of it. We should call Greene and let him know about Morgan's allegations."

"Ted's out of town today," Benczik advised Gideon. "He's expected back tomorrow, and you can call him then. If I get in before you call him tomorrow, I'll make sure to tell Ted exactly what Morgan is claiming. He'll remember this little incident and will confirm that we thought absolutely nothing of seeing Morgan walking in the hallway at the end of the conversation."

The two chatted a bit more about the case and then Gideon walked Benczik to the elevator. Morgan's case was slim at best, and

106

Gideon planned to devote his energies in the near future to preparing a motion to dismiss the case.

18

The two were in the finest restaurant in Washington, D.C. The hors d'oeuvres included grilled jumbo shrimp with a splash of lime and tequila. They split a salad of greens topped with seared peppered tuna, rare in the middle, with a light balsamic vinaigrette dressing. A bottle of Dom Perignon was poured liberally.

The entrees were just as delectable. The two shared a veal chop, pink in the middle, in a Morrel mushroom sauce, and a thinly sliced rare beef, sautéed in a Szechwan sauce. There were new potatoes presented in a bowl on the table, along with a plate of grilled baby vegetables. The two shared a bottle of 1985 California Cabernet Sauvignon.

The feast ended with a raspberry tart and tiramisu. Two decaf cappuccinos were brought steaming hot to the table. The waiter passed around a plate of home baked cookies just for good measure.

Miles had thoroughly enjoyed the meal, and the good company. He had taken an instant liking to Ted Greene when he had met him earlier during the Marvil investigation. Greene had treated Miles and his staff royally, and did so every time he made it to Washington, D.C. This time was no different – except for one thing

– Greene had requested that Miles join him for dinner without his wife. Miles told his wife he had to work late.

"Well, Ted, I've enjoyed this meal, but it seems to me you have something on your mind; otherwise, I would have loved to have brought my wife to enjoy this. What's going on?"

"Ed, I don't know if you have heard, but there is a lawsuit against Western Health Corp. filed by an employee claiming that Marvil was unsafe. You and I both know that the allegations are ridiculous, but I wanted to alert you about them. I suspect that the other side may try to drag you into this, which I would like to avoid. You're a year away from your pension, and I could think of nothing less pleasurable than spending your last year in litigation on the witness stand if this case heats up. We may well get this case dismissed, but if we don't, the other side may try to drag you in on this."

"Ted, I've already been contacted by the other lawyer. I've held off talking to him because I knew we would be getting together. I have absolutely nothing to hide. I think the investigation was done very thoroughly. I think you folks put out a safe drug. I'm going to tell the opposing lawyer that. My guess is that he won't come after me. I did want to meet with you first, however, to let you know, because I think highly of you, and if your lawyers feel differently, I won't say anything."

"Right now, my lawyers are busy in the discovery of this case and planning a motion to dismiss. I want to keep them focused on that, and not on issues like this. I think your approach is fine, Ed.

If you ignore Jacobs, he might feel he's on to something, and he could subpoena you for deposition. If you return his calls and let him know how thorough the investigation was, I suspect he won't go through the time or effort."

Miles by this time had quite a buzz from the Dom Perignon and the Cabernet Sauvignon. He would do exactly as Ted Greene said. He knew that with Greene he had a friend for life, who would treat him and his wife well during their retirement. While he could never put his finger on it, he always had some question as to why the Marvil approval process had gone so much more quickly than others he had coordinated over the years. But he saw no reason, especially as a glass of vintage port was being poured, to rock the boat now.

19

Over the next several weeks, Gideon heard nothing from Jacobs about setting any depositions and had no contact with him at all. Gideon had experienced this phenomenon before: Opposing counsel almost always acted as if they would take a lot of depositions, but they rarely did. In a typical wrongful termination case, the attorney takes the case on a contingency fee basis, meaning that he recovers a specific percentage of any settlement or judgment ultimately received. He does not get paid hourly, and the client generally has to advance all costs of suit. Most clients are quite unwilling to pay the cost of taking a deposition, which could easily be $1,000 a day.

Gideon did receive in the mail, as expected, a request for production of documents. Basically, Jacobs had asked Western Health Corp. to produce all documents related to Marvil and to Morgan's termination from employment. By this point, Gideon had been through these documents on several occasions, and he knew that there was nothing harmful in them. He quickly prepared a response and produced all the documents to Jacobs.

Gideon heard nothing further from Jacobs for months. Greene was starting to get anxious to move the case along, as was

McCabe. The three had lunch and agreed that they had waited long enough to see if Jacobs was going to do any depositions, and that they should immediately prepare a motion to dismiss. Gideon had already begun that process, and it was only a matter of polishing the brief and getting all the supporting papers ready.

Gideon basically planned to make two arguments to the court. The first argument was Morgan had falsified his employment application by failing to disclose his conviction of a felony and, therefore, the whole case should be dismissed. Gideon's second argument was that Morgan had undisputedly been absent excessively, had failed to meet his production goals, failed to improve after being expressly warned in writing and, therefore, had been discharged for good cause. He further observed in the brief that Morgan's only argument to contest the discharge was that Greene somehow suspected that he (Morgan) knew that Marvil was unsafe. Yet, Gideon pointed out that there was absolutely no evidence that Marvil was unsafe and, in fact, the FDA had approved the drug. He also noted that the comment which Morgan alleged to have overheard was so vague and ambiguous that it could not possibly be indicative of some attempt to conceal a defect in Marvil.

Gideon completed the brief and gave it to McCabe to review. McCabe had a few useful comments, and Gideon put in his suggested revisions. He faxed the document to Greene for his comments, and Greene called within two hours. "I've read through this brief," Greene said, "and I think it's excellent. I think we've got a great chance of getting this case kicked."

Gideon knew that he needed to be optimistic with Greene, but also to let him know how difficult motions to dismiss were to get granted. "I think we have a real good shot at this," Gideon responded. "I just hope Judge Farmer doesn't feel some responsibility to let Morgan present his evidence to a jury, even though it is extremely slim."

"This judge has been with us so far," Greene observed, "and I really think he's going to see from your papers what type of person Morgan is. Our company's reputation stands for itself, and I think that might also have a subtle impact on Judge Farmer's thinking." Such extraneous evidence is not supposed to influence a judge, but Gideon knew that Greene had a point. Maybe the fact that Western Health Corp. had been a high-profile company would work in its favor in this case.

Jacobs did a decent job pleading his client's case. Jacobs first argued that Morgan's failure to check the box either yes or no on the employment application with respect to the question, "Have you ever been convicted of a felony?" was simply an oversight. He further argued that a falsification of an employment application would have been if he had checked the box no but did not encompass the situation when an employee simply overlooked a box and failed to check the thing. With respect to whether Western Health Corp. had good cause to terminate Morgan, Jacobs argued that Morgan's absenteeism was explainable by the decline in business at Western Health

Corp., and that Morgan had been absent during other down cycles and had never been disciplined for it. Jacobs also argued that Morgan's lack of productivity was due to the downturn in business. He further stated that the real reason that Morgan was terminated was to cover up the fact that Marvil was unsafe and to keep Morgan from blowing the whistle. He based this argument on the conversation Morgan had overheard and on Morgan's sudden termination by Greene two weeks later.

Gideon filed a reply brief, as permitted by the court rules, which was short and to the point. He argued that Morgan's failure to check the box – whether intentional or not – gave false information to Western Health Corp. If Western Health Corp. been apprised that Morgan had been convicted of a felony, they may have done a more thorough background search and, in fact, may never have hired Morgan in the first place. As to the good cause issue, Gideon argued, in essence, that rules are rules and that Morgan had all but conceded that he had violated them. He also argued that Morgan had not presented a shred of evidence that Marvil was unsafe. He noted that Western Health Corp. had produced all the documents related to the FDA approval procedure of Marvil and that Jacobs could not point to a single document that put into question Marvil's safety.

The hearing before Judge Farmer was scheduled for a Friday afternoon. McCabe, Gideon and Greene walked over to the courthouse and waited patiently for Judge Farmer to take the bench. Judge Farmer was prompt as usual and asked the parties to come

114

forward. He wasted little time with introductions.

"Counsel, I have read all your papers very thoroughly and I have read all the cases you have cited. I view this as a very close case, and I have not made up my mind at all what I am going to do with this motion. I want to hear from each of you briefly. Don't repeat what you put in your papers, but let me know anything else you think might be important in making this determination. Mr. Brown, you go first."

Gideon knew that it would do no good to simply repeat the arguments contained in his papers. Judge Farmer was a quick study, and he no doubt had read the papers thoroughly and knew the law. He decided to argue from the heart. "Your Honor, the reputation of Western Health Corp. has been at stake ever since this lawsuit was filed. That's as it should be, if there is evidence that a company is manufacturing a dangerous drug. But we've been through a lot of litigation now. We're at the point where the plaintiff has had the opportunity to come forward with all the evidence he has. And, Your Honor, when you get down to it, there is simply not a shred of evidence to show that Marvil is unsafe. It's time to put an end to this charade. There is just absolutely nothing to this case."

Judge Farmer listened intently. It appeared to Gideon that he was nodding with approval. There was a long pause.

"Counsel, I agree the evidence is extremely slim in this case," Judge Farmer stated. "If I was sitting on a jury at this point, I would have no choice but to vote in favor of Western Health Corp. But it seems to me that there is some evidence, however, weak, that could lead a different juror to infer that the plaintiff was fired because the company thought he had overheard something about the drug."

"Your Honor," Gideon countered, "that argument would be correct if there was no written documentation justifying Morgan's discharge. But here we have an undisputed record. Morgan admits that he was absent frequently in the six months before his discharge. He admits he was warned in writing and did not improve. He admits that he did not meet his productivity goals. Excessive absenteeism and lack of productivity are grounds, and good grounds, for discharge. Without something more than the vague comment that Morgan allegedly overheard, it is improper to let a jury speculate that Morgan really was terminated to cover up concerns about Marvil's safety. The plaintiff has not produced any evidence from the voluminous records we produced that Marvil was unsafe."

"Well, I do agree that there is only the slimmest of evidence here," Judge Farmer replied. "Let me hear a bit from the plaintiff's counsel. Mr. Jacobs, how do you respond to that?"

"Your Honor, there is enough evidence here to present to a jury. It is extremely difficult for a low-level employee to conclusively establish that a product is unsafe. But we have a lot of circumstantial evidence here. Marvil was shot through the FDA approval procedure in record time. Mr. Morgan had been at the company for years, and he never saw a drug that was approved in such a quick time. He thought there was something fishy. Then, one evening

116

when he was working late and happened to walk past Greene's office, he overheard the conversation which we have set forth in our papers. Granted, it is not an out-and-out admission, but a reasonable jury can infer that there was an argument in Greene's office, a disagreement with whoever else was in there, and that disagreement may have well concerned the safety of Marvil. It should be left to the jury to decide whether the evidence we present establishes that Morgan was discharged wrongfully, or whether the evidence the defendant presents establishes that he was discharged for good cause."

Gideon had never heard Jacobs speak so eloquently or so direct and to the point. Indeed, his papers were not nearly as clear as the two-minute speech he had just given the judge. He felt that the motion was slipping away.

"Well, I am ready to rule," Judge Farmer began. "I have thought long and hard about this case. I have read the papers thoroughly. And as much as I truly believe that the state of the evidence here does not implicate Western Health Corp. at all, I feel compelled to let a jury decide. I am warning you, Mr. Jacobs, that I think it is highly doubtful that any jury will rule in your favor. Perhaps you and Mr. Brown ought to get together after this hearing and see if you can come to some sort of resolution to this case. I am not suggesting any numbers or any terms of settlement, but it seems to me that maybe the company could give Mr. Morgan another chance and reinstate him, and that we all can let bygones be bygones. I'm going to give you two weeks to see if you can settle this case. In the meantime, I am going to deny the motion to dismiss. If you cannot reach a settlement within two weeks, call my clerk, and we're going to set this case for trial within a month thereafter. I am quite sensitive to Mr. Brown's concern about Western Health Corp., and I want all of this resolved as soon as possible. That is my ruling, and I will prepare an order to that effect."

Gideon was extremely disappointed by Judge Farmer's ruling. He felt he had put his best foot forward in the papers and the argument, but in the end, Judge Farmer was simply uneasy about granting the motion. He thought that the judge's comments were helpful, and that he would keep close control of the trial and make rulings that would ultimately favor Western Health Corp. However, it was not the result he wanted to achieve.

Gideon, Greene and McCabe walked back from the courtroom. Unlike the last time they had returned from the court, this time there was not much conversation. They passed the bar that they had stopped at before and did not go in for a drink. The silence was not broken until the three returned to McCabe' office and shut the door.

McCabe initiated the conversation. "Ted, I'm really disappointed that we couldn't get this case dismissed today. But I think we have a good judge. I think that he will do everything in his power to make this trial go well for us. He's simply giving the plaintiff the benefit of the doubt."

Greene was fairly philosophical. "You folks couldn't have

presented the case better. The judge was just feeling some sympathy for Morgan. I'm sure it's all going to turn out fine when we try it."

"I hate to raise this, Ted," McCabe continued. "But I ought to at least discuss with you the possibility of settling this case. Judge Farmer, as you heard, has asked us to try to do that in the next two weeks. What is your position on settlement?"

Gideon could see Greene's hostility building. "Nothing against Judge Farmer or you, Bart, but there is absolutely no way that we are going to settle this case. Morgan is plainly full of shit. This case has gotten too much publicity. If we settle this case, they will hound us about Marvil forever. I'm not afraid of any jury, and I'm not going to settle. Let's just get ready for trial."

"I'm completely with you, Ted," McCabe responded. "We're going to break our ass to win this thing. Gideon, call Jacobs tomorrow and tell him that we're not settling. Then make a conference call to Judge Farmer's clerk. Tell him to put us on the trial calendar as quickly as possible and start preparing for trial immediately."

20

Gonzales had been at Western Health Corp. for nearly six months. It was not uncommon for an undercover operation to take so long. An undercover operative could not simply go into the workforce and immediately begin snooping around. He had to develop the trust of his co-workers and his peers. He needed to set the stage very carefully.

The first couple of months, Gonzales confined himself mostly to knowing and meeting others in the mailroom. Part of his job was to deliver the mail to all the offices at the Western Health Corp. site. In the process, he began over time to develop a feel for the different Western Health Corp. workers and their assignments. While he had come to Western Health Corp. under the guise of learning about their marketing, he soon began to realize that he needed to get to know individuals in other departments in order to try to find the person or persons who might give him some necessary information for his case.

One evening, Gonzales was in the office working late. He had been invited to attend a marketing meeting from 5 to 7 that evening and was now sorting the internal mail which would be delivered the next morning. There were scarcely any other employees present at that time. Gonzales was about to leave when the phone in the mailroom rang. He thought that was odd. Who would be calling the mail-room at 9:00 p.m. in the evening?

Gonzales picked up the line. The voice on the other end was muffled. "I know who you are, and why you are at Western Health Corp. I'm not in a position to talk to you yet. But stick around. You're gonna find what your boss wants."

21

A surprise was in store for Gideon when he returned to work the next morning. Jacobs had personally served a notice setting the deposition of Ted Greene, Alex Benczik and Ben Williams. He had set the depositions all for one day, meaning that he only planned to ask questions to each witness for about two hours. It was an indication, however, that Jacobs was planning to ready his case for trial.

Gideon called Greene to confirm that each witness would be available on the date noticed for the deposition. Greene assured Gideon that everyone would change their calendar if necessary, but that they wanted this case to get moving and not to have any further delays. Gideon arranged a meeting to prepare each of the witnesses for the deposition two days before the depositions were scheduled. In the meantime, Gideon sent each of the witnesses a packet of documents which he thought were relevant to their testimony and which they might see at some point during their deposition.

Gideon went out to Western Health Corp. the next week for a full day of witness preparation. He decided that he would begin the preparation session with each of the witnesses there to hear his general instructions about answering deposition questions. After he finished that process, he would speak to each of them individually about their own testimony. This was important because each of the three witnesses only knew certain facts about the case, and Jacobs would have to ask all the right questions to make sure he got all the information. If the witnesses overheard conversations about the other witnesses' testimony, they might be inclined to testify about facts that they really knew little about.

Gideon spent about a half hour with the three, giving them general instructions about the deposition. He emphasized that they needed to listen to every question carefully and to only answer the direct question posed. Too often, witnesses do not listen carefully to questions, and end up answering things that the lawyer never asked and often end up giving damaging testimony. He always liked to give the example of the witness who was asked, "Did you have breakfast this morning?" Rather than answering yes, and making the lawyer ask the next question, the typical witness would say, "Yes, I had coffee, toast and eggs." While this always got a chuckle from the person Gideon was telling this to, the point was well made. Just answer the question that is asked – no more, no less.

Gideon always told his witnesses that the most important thing to do was to tell the truth during their deposition. If they told the truth, they would not find themselves boxed into a corner by tricky questions or getting defensive. Most witnesses get themselves into trouble when they stretch the truth a little bit and are caught later with an inconsistency. Gideon impressed upon all three witnesses how confident he was about their handling of the case so far, and how he saw little that Jacobs could get through these depositions.

Gideon then met with each witness individually. With Greene, he went over the circumstances of Morgan's termination. Greene told Gideon that Williams had gone to him about six months before the termination and said that he had a problem employee. Greene recounted to Gideon the fact that he and Williams had sat down and decided to issue a written warning and to develop a specific performance plan aimed at increasing Morgan's production.

Gideon also reviewed with Greene Morgan's testimony about what he overheard in Greene's office about two weeks before he was terminated. Greene confirmed that he and Benczik were having a conversation in the office, and that the entire thrust of the conversation was that Benczik needed to get a lot of work done for the FDA, nothing sinister as Morgan had insinuated.

Finally, the two went over the final conversation between Greene and Morgan. They reviewed Greene's notes in detail to ensure that Greene's recollection was consistent with what was contained in the notes. All in all, the meeting went quite well, and Gideon was confident that Greene would make a fine witness.

The next meeting was with Benczik. Benczik, too, seemed quite self-assured about the deposition. He described for Gideon in painstaking detail the work he had done on Marvil and the documentation he had prepared for the FDA. They reviewed as many of his notes as they could, and then moved on to the conversation with

Greene that Morgan had overheard. Benczik again recounted the conversation, confirming what Greene had said just an hour before.

Gideon was sure that Jacobs would be at a complete disadvantage in asking any scientific questions about Marvil because of Benczik's obvious expertise in the area. Given the soundproof nature of the documentation, he could not conceive that Jacobs would get very far in this examination.

The final witness was Williams. Gideon spent extra time with Williams going over the general instructions he had given before each of the three witnesses. Gideon had recalled that from his initial conversation with Williams, Williams tended to ramble on about issues, and he wanted to make sure that Williams knew not to volunteer information. He did some practice question and answer sessions designed to get Williams comfortable at answering questions. Although Williams did run on in his answers to some of the questions, as a whole, his performance was adequate. Gideon stressed with Williams that it was perfectly okay for him to say that he did not recall something, or to review the warnings in the file and other information if he had trouble remembering things. He left the meeting a bit uneasy as to how Williams would perform, but not all that concerned since Greene had made the final decision and Benczik was the expert as to the safety of Marvil.

The depositions took place in Jacob's office two days later. Jacobs was a solo practitioner, and his office was not very impressive. He shared a secretary with several other lawyers, and his conference room was quite small. It was warm, and uncomfortable for the witnesses. Jacobs did not offer any of the witnesses any coffee or any of the other amenities one usually expects during a deposition. Gideon knew it would be a long day. Gideon had asked Jacobs to depose Greene first so that Greene could get back to work. Jacobs had kindly agreed, and Greene was the first witness to take the oath. Williams and Benczik were not present during the testimony and waited in the outside reception area.

Jacobs began the deposition by asking Greene about his educational and employment background. Greene detailed his education, culminating in an MBA at 24, and his quick rise through Western Health Corp. Jacobs then asked Greene to explain what his duties as the president of the company were. Greene said he had his hands in virtually everything, ranging from employment decisions to receiving reports on laboratory work and FDA approval. Jacobs then launched into a series of questions which, for the first time, were aimed at questioning the safety of Marvil.

Q: "Mr. Greene, how many drugs have gone through the FDA approval process since you began at Western Health Corp.?"

A: "Literally dozens."

Q: "And of all these drugs that received FDA approval, which drug took the shortest time for the FDA to review?"

A: "Marvil."

Q: "How long did it take for the entire FDA process to approve Marvil?"

A: "Approximately one year."

Q: "And of all the other drugs that you have seen go through the FDA approval process, how long was the next shortest FDA approval process?"

A: "I would have to look at the records, but I would estimate three years."

Q: "Of all the drugs you have seen through the FDA approval process, has there ever been any drug other than Marvil in which the safety was questioned?"

A: "No, this is the very first time."

Q: "And isn't it true, sir, at the time that Marvil was approved by the FDA, your company's profits had begun to flatten out and you wanted that drug on the market quick?"

A: "I did want the drug on the market quick, but I was not concerned about profits. Sure, we had flattened out a little bit, but we were still an extremely profitable company. I wanted that drug on the market because we truly believed and still believe that this was a revolutionary drug that could help a number of people. If you're insinuating that we cut any corners in order to make a profit, I flatly deny it. The records clearly show the contrary."

Gideon decided that is was an appropriate time at this point to take a break from the deposition. While Greene's testimony was fine, he could see Greene getting angry and defensive. He wanted to reassure Greene that Jacobs really had very little to go on before Greene got angrier and perhaps said something that he shouldn't.

"Let's take a five-minute break and stretch our legs; we've been going close to an hour," Gideon stated. And with those words, he and Greene walked out of the deposition room.

Greene had lost some of his cool. "His whole theory is just bullshit," Greene told Gideon. "He simply twisted the facts. This drug was so marketable that I did press Benczik to speed it through the FDA approval process. It was just something that was desperately needed, and I wanted it out on the market."

"Ted, that is clearly a point that you want to make and make forcefully when you testify at trial. But you need to do it in a less defensive manner. I think you're going to make Jacobs look like a fool given all the documentation that we have and the FDA's ringing endorsement of Marvil. Just don't let him get to you."

Greene calmed down considerably. "I appreciate your calling time out, Gideon," Greene remarked. "I've been through this before, and I should know better. I promise I'll keep my cool. It's just that he is impugning my integrity, and the integrity of the company I worked so hard to build." Gidcon was supportive and told Greene that he completely understood how he was feeling. That was one of the unfortunate side effects of litigation, Gideon noted.

When the deposition resumed, Greene was much more in control. In fact, Jacobs was beginning to get frustrated by Greene's answers. Greene's knowledge of the company was outstanding, and he had a keen memory. He gave a blow-by-blow description of his efforts with Williams to counsel Morgan and to make sure that he improved. He also went through a detailed description of his meeting with Morgan prior to terminating him. Jacobs was scoring absolutely no points.

Jacobs then got to the evening when Morgan overheard the conversation in his office. Greene handled this line of questioning deftly.

Q: "Do you recall seeing Morgan walk by your office about two weeks before his termination late one evening?"

A: "Yes, I do."

Q: "Who was in your office at that time?"

A: "Alex Benczik."

Q: "Would you characterize the meeting as friendly or unfriendly?"

Mr. Brown: "Objection. Calls for speculation. The term 'friendly or unfriendly' is vague and ambiguous."

Mr. Jacobs: "I'll rephrase, Counsel. Did you raise your voice at any time during the meeting?"

A: "Yes, I did. I raised my voice not because I was angry or upset, but because I wanted to get my point across to Mr. Benczik that we are in the homestretch, that there was a lot of work to be done, but that I wanted it completed so that we could get the drug on the market. I also told Mr. Benczik, by the way, that I had recognized his extraordinary efforts, and that I would give him a long vacation when he completed the task."

Q: "Did Mr. Benczik register any concern or objection about

the speed in which you had asked him to ready Marvil for FDA approval?"

A: "No, Benczik did not have any objection. The only concern, if that's what you want to call it, was how hard he was working and whether he could get it all done. But he had no concern at all about our getting Marvil on the market. He was confident about the tests he had performed, and so was I."

Q: "Did he tell you that he had any doubts about the safety of Marvil?"

A:" No, sir, absolutely not."

Greene had performed quite well. Jacobs was clearly getting frustrated. Normally, Gideon would interject with more than an occasional objection, but Greene was handling himself so well that he let the questioning continue. Jacobs fared no better when he tried to link Morgan's termination to the evening in which he overheard the conversation. Greene stated emphatically that he had been aware of Morgan's performance problems six months prior to that event, and that he and Williams had developed a specific plan to try to have Morgan improve his performance.

Morgan had been expressly warned in writing about his performance deficiencies, but had not changed his conduct. Greene flatly denied that the conversation Morgan heard had anything to do with his termination.

With that testimony, Jacobs wrapped up Greene's deposition. He asked that Benczik be summoned to begin his deposition.

Gideon and Greene stepped into the hallway. Gideon expected to bid Greene farewell and to speak to him later that day. Greene, however, was clearly pumped up about the day's events and decided to stay for the depositions.

"I want to hear what Jacobs has up his sleeve, and I think it'll make our guys feel more comfortable if I'm there," Greene told Gideon. "Is there any problem with me being in the deposition?"

Gideon told Greene that he had the right as the company representative to witness the deposition, and that he was sure Jacobs would not have any objections.

Gideon gave Benczik a few last encouraging words, and they walked together into the deposition. Benczik was sworn in by the court reporter, and Greene took a seat next to Gideon. Jacobs began his examination questioning Benczik as to his scientific background. Benczik listed a whole series of degrees and awards that he had received. He named a dozen articles in various journals that he had published about his lab work and various chemicals.

Jacobs was to find no hole in Benczik's credentials.

Jacobs then put a number of documents before Benczik. They were his handwritten notes regarding various testing procedures about Marvil. Gideon got the impression that Jacobs was doing this more for educational purposes than to uncover any flaws in the testing. Perhaps Jacobs thought that if he was conversant with the terminology at trial, the jury might believe that his client actually knew something. Again, he made absolutely no headway with

Benczik.

Gideon was extremely pleased with the way Benczik handled questioning. Unlike Greene, he did not even have a moment where he got defensive or appeared a bit flustered. Everything Jacobs threw at him, Benczik handled with ease. Jacobs tried to trip Benczik up about the timing of the FDA approval process of Marvil.

Q: "Marvil was approved by the FDA faster than any drug while you were at the company, isn't that correct?"

A: "I believe that is so."

Q: "Did you feel uncomfortable with the rate at which you were asked to get FDA approval of Marvil?"

A: "No, I did not feel uncomfortable at all. The only thing I felt was a bit overworked because of the amount of documentation I needed to prepare for the FDA."

Q: "Did you have any doubts about the safety of Marvil?"

A: "Absolutely not, sir."

Q: "Did you ever have an argument with Greene about the FDA process?"

A: "No, I did not."

Q: "Then why did Greene raise his voice at you during the conversation that my client overheard?"

A: "Counsel, it had absolutely nothing to do with the safety of Marvil. Ted can be quite demanding, and I felt he was asking a lot of me. We had some discussion about it. I was tired. But I respected his desire to get the product on the market, and one could hardly quarrel with the result."

Jacobs was getting nowhere fast. Benczik was Gideon's strongest witness, and Jacobs began to realize that he ought not waste his time with any more questions. He quickly concluded Benczik's deposition and asked that Williams be sent in for his deposition.

The depositions had been going for about four hours. Gideon was hungry and thought it would be good to have a little extra preparation for Williams, his most problematic witness.

Jacobs agreed, and Gideon and the three Western Health Corp. officials went out to lunch. Gideon commended Benczik on his testimony and worked with Williams again on keeping his responses short. Greene was pleased enough with the way things had gone that he decided to take off after lunch.

"I've seen enough. I don't think Jacobs is going to get anywhere. I might as well get back to the salt mines." Benczik also indicated that he wanted to get back to work as well.

Gideon and Williams went back for the afternoon deposition. Williams performed better than expected, though not spectacularly. On occasion, he contradicted himself as to the course of action he took against Morgan. Much of this was correctable, and Gideon was sure that on direct examination with documents in front of him and with friendly questioning, Williams would perform adequately. He followed Gideon's instructions and did not answer questions in too verbose a fashion. When it came down to the performance problems of Morgan, Williams was very specific and to the point. He also described in great detail his caution in going to Greene to ask for advice on how to deal with Morgan, and their discussions on how to try to get Morgan to improve. He testified that he wanted Morgan to succeed and issued the warning to Morgan to let him know unequivocally that he needed to straighten up. He had tried to talk to Morgan on several occasions during the months after the warning to see if there was anything he could do to help, but Morgan was unresponsive. Finally, he asked Greene to intercede to try to talk some sense into Morgan. He had not been at the meeting with Greene, but had heard the story from Greene shortly thereafter. He knew that the company then had no choice but to terminate Morgan.

Jacobs then concluded the deposition. Gideon went back to the office and reviewed his notes. All in all, the witnesses had performed quite well. The depositions would be of no use to Jacobs. In fact, the experience of testifying under oath would probably make each of the witnesses more at ease at trial. Gideon had increasingly begun to view Benczik as his best witness, especially in view of the fact that he ran rings around Jacobs with his scientific knowledge. If Gideon could convince the jury that Benczik was in charge and was sure that there was nothing wrong with Marvil, he had a good chance of winning the case.

With the case nearing for trial, Gideon prepared full blast for trial. He did a cross-examination outline of Morgan, and prepared his direct examinations of Greene, Benczik and Williams. His

134

tentative plan was to call Greene as the first witness, sandwich Williams in the middle, and finish up strong with Benczik's scientific testimony. That way, he would have a good first and last witness.

Gideon had little discussions with Greene or anyone else at Western Health Corp. over the next several weeks. He had told them that they would do intensive trial preparation a week before the trial was scheduled. The Monday before the trial was to begin, Gideon got to the office early and planned to call Greene first thing. The message light was flashing. The message was from Greene. It was shocking. "Gideon, I've got terrible news. Alex Benczik has been murdered."

PART II

1

The average salary of a partner at Longworth & Drucker was approximately $800,000 per year. The road to partnership was an arduous one. Each year, forty or more new lawyers from the best law schools in the country started at Longworth & Drucker. All had exceptional grades in law school; all were ambitious. All were expected to bill 50-60 hours per week; many billed more.

Of these forty individuals, one or two would make partner at the firm. Many would leave on their own volition; others would be asked to leave. Still others would be asked to stay at the firm, given a special title and more money, but would not be partners. In the past several years, more associates at Longworth & Drucker were being placed in such special positions than making partner. In that special role, the lawyer would make about $200,000 per year – more money than if he went elsewhere and were a partner in virtually any other firm. However, the lawyer would not have any role in the firm's decision-making. The lawyer would still report to the partners. For most, however, the money was simply too attractive to pass up.

Gideon had a year left before the partnership decision would be made with respect to him. He had mixed emotions about the whole process. He had stayed with the firm for six years because part of him wanted very much to be a partner. He hoped that it would give him more of an opportunity to play a mentor role to younger lawyers. He was absolutely mortified how some partners treated the lawyers at the firm and vowed that he would never act in that fashion.

There was another part of Gideon that really did not want to stay with the firm. While the money was attractive, it really did not mean all that much to him. As luck would have it, Gideon had done well in the real estate market in Los Angeles and currently owned a nice home. He had been able to save quite a bit of his $100,000 plus per year salary during his time at Longworth & Drucker. In addition, both Gideon's and Ali's families were quite well off. He knew that money would never be an issue. For that reason, he had little interest in staying on with the firm if his workload remained the same. Because of the decline in the economy, Gideon knew that the firm was increasingly requiring its partners to bill more and more hours and to bring in business. The days of becoming a partner and kicking back were over.

He had seen some extremes among associates in their drive to make partner. Some decided that the way to partnership was to forego all vacations altogether and to work virtually non-stop. Others tried to get in close with a particularly influential senior partner. Still others turned their efforts toward bringing in new business. Gideon certainly worked hard, made efforts to bring in new business and tried to play the political game in the firm when possible. But he had other interests and wanted to start a family; he simply did not want to give his whole life to the firm.

Ali had mixed emotions about the whole process as well. On the one hand, she certainly enjoyed the steady stream of income. Gideon and Ali had no worries about money whatsoever. While neither lived an extravagant life, they never had to be concerned whether something cost too much. It was a comfortable and pleasant existence. On the other hand, Ali tired of Gideon's long hours and his frequently voicing frustration about the politics at the law firm. Sometimes she thought he would be much happier either teaching law or practicing law on his own. Of course, that would mean some modification in their stream of income and, potentially, a bit of belt tightening.

The Western Health Corp. case would obviously have an impact on Gideon's prospects for partnership. This was a new client that the firm had long tried to obtain. Success in the trial would undoubtedly bring more business and would raise Gideon's reputation in the eyes of the partners of the firm. None of this escaped Gideon, but he tried not to let this bring any more pressure to bear on him. It was tough enough readying for trial in a case in which the company stood a chance of losing an enormous sum of money.

Although Gideon had talked about the partnership issue with his wife on a number of occasions, the issue was never discussed at work. McCabe, the partner on the Western Health Corp. case and the partner whom Gideon worked for the most during the past several years, never even alluded to the issue. This frustrated Gideon, because he would have liked to have known that McCabe would be a strong supporter of him when the partnership decision came up. While he felt that McCabe would be such a supporter, sometimes he simply did not know. The way to get McCabe firmly in his camp, Gideon thought, was to win the Western Health Corp. case.

Gideon would have been dismayed to know that McCabe had simply not given the issue much thought. McCabe himself was angling towards a more powerful role in the firm. As a senior partner and head of a department in the firm, McCabe certainly had considerable influence with his partners. It was not a secret, however, that McCabe was ambitious in his own right. Much of McCabe's rainmaking efforts were plainly designed to get the attention of his other partners. McCabe wanted to be the next head of the firm.

It had been a coup for McCabe to get Western Health Corp.'s business, and he was increasingly becoming anxious about the outcome of the lawsuit. While McCabe and Ted Greene had become quite close, McCabe was concerned that if the jury hit Western Health Corp. hard, Greene might take his business elsewhere. McCabe became obsessed with keeping Greene happy, showering him with tickets in every sport and expensive dinners. Gideon was included in some, but not all, of these meetings. This got Gideon angry, because he had developed a good rapport with Greene, and felt that McCabe was positioning himself to take full credit for the trial if it went in Western Health Corp.'s favor. Gideon had worked his tail off since the beginning of the case, and he wanted to reap the fruits of any victory that might occur.

Allen Henderson, the junior associate who had helped McCabe briefly in preparing subpoenas for Morgan's medical records, also began playing a more prominent role in the case. Any time a case goes to trial, there is a massive amount of work to be done. McCabe reviewed much of the written material but did not do anything on his own. That left Gideon with the lion's share of the work, but he needed assistance. Henderson was eager and willing to help. He was a quick study, and soon knew as much about the case as Gideon. He and Gideon hit it off, often talking long into the night about many issues other than work. Both Henderson and Gideon were married and faced many of the same issues at home regarding their long hours. Both of their wives were impatient about the long hours and were critical of their respective husbands for allowing the firm to control their destiny.

Although Henderson talked frequently about staying at the firm only a few years, Gideon knew that Henderson deep down wanted desperately to succeed. For that reason, Gideon had taken Henderson under his wing and had tried to build Henderson's confidence in his legal skills. Henderson was very smart; unfortunately, he was unsure of himself. Gideon felt that some lawyers sensed this and did not respect Henderson as much as they should. Gideon had set out some time ago to help Henderson in this area, and he felt that his efforts showed some dividends.

Henderson had handled several cases quite successfully, and the partners appeared to take some notice. Perhaps Henderson's role on the Western Health Corp. case would further his career as well.

2

With the trial only a week away and Alex Benczik being murdered, the obvious move was for Western Health Corp. to ask for a short continuance of the trial. Gideon needed to regroup and consider his trial strategy, and Judge Farmer, under the circumstances, had no difficulty with the request. He continued the trial for two weeks upon Gideon's request. The police, in the meantime, were investigating the murder of Benczik. In fact, the day that Ted Greene called with the news, McCabe and Gideon drove up to Western Health Corp. to provide any assistance they could. When they arrived, the police were on the scene. They had questioned all those who knew Benczik, including Ben Williams and Ted Greene. The police also were interested in questioning Gideon and McCabe. Gideon was glad that McCabe had accompanied him, because he felt that a partner ought to be present if the police were questioning the lawyers regarding the murder. McCabe controlled the meeting with the police. He was direct and definitive with all his answers. It did not seem that the police viewed any lawyer from Longworth & Drucker as a suspect, but one could never be sure. McCabe detailed to the police the firm's involvement with Western Health Corp., and stated that the firm had viewed Benczik as a key and helpful witness to the defense. McCabe further explained that the firm had been so dismayed by Benczik's sudden death that it had to ask for a continuance of the trial. Nothing about Benczik's death was at all helpful to the defense.

The police took all of McCabe's comments down in detail. They did not ask any questions of Gideon, and Gideon was sure that McCabe would not let him speak if asked any questions. Longworth & Drucker took very seriously its reputation as being an ethical law firm, and any public comments were carefully marshaled by the partners.

At the close of the meeting, McCabe asked the police officers whether they had any suspects. The police were baffled; they thought Benczik's death was connected to the case, but they had very few leads. Gideon had been dying to talk during the entire meeting but had held his thoughts inside. He asked McCabe to step out, however, before the police left.

In the hallway, Gideon told McCabe what he had been thinking. "Bart, I know this sounds farfetched, but Morgan must have known that Benczik's testimony was the death knell to his case. He was such a credible and thorough witness, that the jury would certainly have felt that Marvil was safe. Who else had such a strong motive to kill Benczik than Morgan? I think we need to tell the police about that issue and let them do the investigation for themselves."

McCabe was embarrassed because he had not thought of that prospect. "I think you are absolutely right, Gideon, I should have thought of that myself. Let's both of us go back in there and mention it to the police. I think we need to be very careful about accusing the other side at this point, because Jacobs may well seize that issue and go to the press claiming that we're trying to discredit his client. I want to avoid any implication that we are trying to get an unfair advantage by all this."

McCabe was clearly right. But Gideon felt in the pit of his stomach that perhaps Morgan had gone over the deep end again. They decided to go back into the room and advise the police officers of their thoughts. The police were thankful for their thoughts and promised to follow up on it. The police then left the premises without further questioning.

McCabe and Gideon took Greene out to lunch. Greene was visibly shaken. "This is just a tragedy," Greene said. "Benczik was our most valued scientist, he is irreplaceable. Not to mention that he was our strongest witness for this trial. Does this change the case in your view?" Greene asked.

Before Gideon could open his mouth, McCabe chimed in. "Obviously, Ted, a key witness of ours has been killed. However, Gideon has told me that his deposition was quite good, and we can read to the jury his deposition testimony. While live testimony is always better, the jury may well, under the circumstances, place even more credence on Benczik's testimony. All in all, although we obviously wish this did not happen, I don't think this changes our strategy in this case."

Greene was pleased to hear all this. "I'll tell you, Bart, when I heard the news, my first thought was to try to settle this case and just get rid of it. As I am sure you know, that is completely the opposite of what I want to do in this case, but I thought my back was against the wall. It makes sense what you're saying, and I think that the best course is just to go forward with this case as if nothing happened."

The three finished lunch, and McCabe and Gideon bid their goodbyes to Greene. The ride back to the office was eerie. Neither McCabe nor Gideon talked for virtually the entire trip. Both knew that they would have to change the entire strategy of the case now that Benczik was dead. While reading a deposition to the jury would have some value, there is nothing like having a live witness the jury can see and believe. Clearly, the defense needed to regroup.

Finally, after what seemed to be an interminable time, Gideon spoke first. "Bart, I think this changes our plan in the trial. I had thought all along that Benczik would be our strongest witness, and that we would close our case with him. That obviously has got to change. What we should do, I think, is read the deposition of Benczik to the jury first off. I think we then could go with Williams as our second witness, trying to minimize any inconsistencies in our testimony. It's now clear that Greene is the key witness for us. He should be our last witness, and we're going to have to prep him long and hard. This whole case is going to turn on whether the jury believes Greene's testimony."

"I agree," McCabe said. "Ted Greene is a very likeable guy, and the jury will pick up on that. I think you're analyzing the case in the right fashion, Gideon, there's really no other choice. Just make sure you prepare Greene over and over again so that he doesn't make an ass of himself." McCabe was never one to pull punches. At a time where Gideon was feeling a bit unsure of what to do next, McCabe had made it quite clear that the ball was in Gideon's court, and if Greene was not a good witness, it would be Gideon's fault. Gideon didn't really appreciate this added pressure, but knew that that was how things worked at Longworth & Drucker. Gideon vowed to make Greene the star witness.

3

As the trial neared, the police made no headway whatsoever in their investigation into Alex Benczik's murder. There were no eyewitnesses to the murder; it apparently took place quite late at night in the Western Health Corp. building. What Benczik was working on was a mystery; Greene was aware of several of Benczik's projects, but none had any imminent deadlines. He thought it was strange that Benczik was around the office so late in the evening.

Morgan apparently had been questioned at length by the police. He did not have an alibi for the evening in question – he claimed he was alone at home preparing for the trial. Nobody, however, could place Morgan anywhere near Western Health Corp. on that evening.

Benczik had no family to speak of. As a man who had devoted his entire life to scientific research, he had little interest in the trappings of married life. He rarely, if ever, dated, and had few hobbies. This was not the type of person who would have enemies with a motive to kill. The police also had ruled out burglary as any reason for the murder. Western Health Corp. had not been ransacked, and there appeared to be nothing missing. The Western Health Corp. trial would go forward with no solution to the murder of Alex

Benczik.

Judge Farmer had been quite clear with both Gideon and Jacobs that there would be no mention of the unfortunate circumstances of Benczik's death and its proximity to trial. Gideon would certainly be allowed to read Benczik's deposition testimony to the jury. The only thing the jury would hear, from the Judge, was that Benczik had passed away before the trial. Farmer warned that if either Jacobs or Gideon tried to take advantage of Benczik's death by making comments to the jury, he would declare an immediate mistrial. He would also cite the offender for contempt. Farmer was a man of his word, and neither Gideon nor Jacobs were inclined to cross him.

As the trial date approached, Gideon was amazed as to how those around him seemed to change. McCabe, who scarcely ever got involved in the way Gideon managed his cases, was calling Gideon or stopping in his office a dozen times a day. He wanted hourly reports about witness preparation, Gideon's intent on how to cross-examine Morgan, the order of witnesses Gideon intended to call, and everything else that was going on in the trial. It was apparent that McCabe wanted desperately to win the trial so that more Western Health Corp. business would come his way. Although McCabe never said anything directly to Gideon, he implied on several occasions that Greene was likely to steer a major corporate deal to Longworth & Drucker if things went well in the trial.

Allen Henderson, the junior associate who had helped Gideon

early in the case and was assisting in much of the written preparation for trial, also seemed to have a different mindset. Gideon sensed Henderson felt that the partners would take notice of his work on such a high-profile case. While Henderson was a long way from the partnership rat race, he had long sought recognition from someone other than Gideon and felt that this was his big chance. Indeed, Henderson's work had been superb; not only was it done on time, but it needed little revision. Gideon was always one to pass on compliments about younger associates if they did good work, and he made sure that McCabe knew about Henderson's performance.

Even Ali seemed to take a greater interest in Gideon's work than usual. Often, Gideon simply steered clear of long-winded discussions about his cases, leaving only the most interesting ones the topics of discussion. Now, the minute he would get home, he would be virtually assaulted by Ali with questions. What did Gideon intend to focus on during opening statement? What type of jurors was he looking for? Was he going to do a long cross-examination of Morgan, or was he simply going to try to make his points and get out? For the first time, Ali spoke freely about what would happen if Gideon made partner. They probably would not move from the house right away, but maybe they would start looking for a bigger home. Perhaps Gideon would replace his little sports car with a fancier European sedan. A nice trip would not be a bad idea, either.

Gideon, too, obviously understood the magnitude of the case. If he got a defense verdict on such a high-profile case, the firm would be hard-pressed not to make him partner. Losing, of course, would not spell the end of his chances, but it certainly could not help. Gideon tried to keep these thoughts out of his mind and focus only on trial strategy, but naturally they crept in now and then.

Only Ted Greene appeared to remain his calm and cool self. Gideon spent long hours with Greene preparing his testimony. Greene now was the key witness in the case. He would be Gideon's closing witness. It would all come down to Greene. If the jury believed Greene, Morgan would lose his case. If the jury at all felt that Greene was retaliating against Morgan, it would be a disaster. A multimillion-dollar verdict was not out of the question. Even with such high stakes, Greene never wavered in his recollection or in the persuasiveness of his testimony.

There was not even a hint of the defensiveness that had emerged during Greene's deposition testimony on one or two occasions. The true test, of course, would come at trial. But Gideon was pleased at Greene's resiliency as he barraged Greene with questions during practice cross-examination.

By the time Gideon had finished preparing Greene for the final time, it was after 11:00 p.m. the Friday evening before the trial scheduled to begin on Monday. Gideon had warned Ali that he was likely to be home quite late. When he arrived home at about midnight, the lights were out in the house; Ali was fast asleep. Gideon fumbled around in the dark and hung up his clothes. He was wide awake. He knew there was no reason to even pretend to try to fall asleep. He went out to the den and put on the television.

Nothing on TV caught his attention. He was quite restless. He decided to catch up on the bills. They were kept in the nightstand next to Ali. He went quietly back into the bedroom and opened up the drawer. He groped around for the bills and picked up a handful of envelopes. He felt something hard on the bottom of the drawer. He picked it up and ran out into the lit hallway. He could not believe his eyes - it was a Colt 45 revolver - the same type of gun that had killed Alex Benczik.

4

Gideon could not sleep at all. What the hell was Ali doing with a Colt 45 revolver? He knew his imagination was racing – Colt 45 revolvers are very common, there are millions floating around Los Angeles. But why would Ali conceivably have a gun? Gideon found it especially appalling because the two had often talked about their opposition to the National Rifle Association and their strong support for handgun control. Ali was as liberal as they came, and certainly had no need for a gun.

Gideon kept a watchful eye on Ali as it became morning. He was looking for some sign that she was awake. Finally, at about 8:30, Ali turned toward him. "You must have got in real late last night, Gideon, did everything go okay?" She obviously did not know what Gideon had discovered. About ten times, Gideon started to raise the subject; but as hard as he could try, he simply could not confront Ali. There had to be some good explanation, Gideon thought. Maybe Ali had gotten scared and simply wanted some protection because Gideon had been coming home late so much. That must be it, Gideon thought to himself. He would feel silly if he confronted Ali with his wild thoughts. Still, he could not understand why Ali would not have mentioned the fact that she wanted a gun in the house. Perhaps Ali knew how much Gideon opposed guns, and simply wanted to avoid a fight during such a time of tension in Gideon's life. That seemed like Ali. She would not want to divert Gideon's attention from the case and bother him with such an issue. She probably just went ahead and got the gun and thought that Gideon would never find it. That's why she had hidden it so carefully in her drawer.

Even though it was Saturday, with the trial just two days away, Gideon planned to work the entire day. He had a cup of coffee with Ali, and quickly got into the car and sped on the freeway to work. Allen Henderson was already there waiting with a number of documents that he had prepared. Gideon had asked Henderson to prepare a part of his opening statement - which gave a brief description of the history of Western Health Corp. and its rise in the bio-technology field. Henderson's summary of Western Health Corp. was excellent; Gideon could hardly imagine where Henderson had picked up so many details. It is hard to get such information just from a review of the cold documents.

"Allen, this is just terrific," Gideon told his colleague. "Where did you get all this information from? Frankly, I didn't even know half of this stuff."

Henderson enjoyed the compliment, but recoiled a bit at Gideon's questioning. "Well," Henderson began, looking for the right words, "I took it upon myself a couple of weeks ago to take a ride out to Western Health Corp. I figured they would probably have some up-to-date promotional material that we did not have a copy of. I didn't want to bother anyone up there, and I remembered that you had the keys to the building. I just borrowed them and went up late one evening and looked through the material. I was right. The most recent promotional material contained a lot of information that I knew would be helpful in preparing both the opening and closing statements."

While Gideon admired Henderson's initiative, he was a bit miffed that Henderson had not advised him of his plans. Gideon always made clear to the people who worked with him that he encouraged them to be creative in any project given; he made it equally clear, however, that he wanted to be informed of anything being done on his cases. Gideon knew that he was ultimately responsible to the partner in any given case, and it was often embarrassing for a partner to come in and question the amount of time spent on a particular project by a younger associate. Gideon always kept close tabs on the work done and demanded constant feedback.

"Allen, I think that your idea was terrific. But I'm pretty pissed. You shouldn't be going in my desk, for one. And, you know that I want to be kept informed about things. I probably would have given you the go ahead, but can you imagine if Ted Greene was there working late and saw you lurking around the office? It could have blown our whole chance of getting more Western Health Corp. business."

"You just have been so under the gun, Gideon, that I didn't want to bother you with such a trivial thing. I thought that if I did this on my own and put out a good work product, it would show you that I'm ready to take on more responsibility."

Gideon knew that Henderson was sensitive about his work and was trying desperately to show his lawyering skills. He felt bad that he had hit such a sore spot with Henderson. Still, it struck Gideon as odd that Henderson would go out to Western Health Corp. without telling him. Gideon wanted some more information. "When exactly did you go out there, Allen? I mean, I'm not being critical, but it may well be that Ted will want to know where I got the information, and I'm going to be honest with him. As you know, Ted gave me the green light to go out there at any time, and I'll tell him that because I was so busy, I gave you the keys and asked you to go out there. I know he'll understand. But I don't want to make up a story to Greene as to how we got the information."

"Oh, well, I don't recall exactly, but it was several weeks ago. I'm almost certain it was before we got the continuance. You had mentioned to me about doing the piece for the opening statement, and with the trial right around the corner, I figured I'd better get going on it. Little did I know that the trial would be continued, and that I didn't need to get it done on a rush basis."

Gideon figured it was time to drop the issue. "Listen, Allen, the bottom line is that you did a great job on this. That's what I'm going to remember. Don't take any offense by this. Just run things by me the next time, okay?" Henderson nodded, and asked if there was anything else he could do to prepare for the trial. Gideon told him that he had done more than enough, that he ought to spend the rest of the weekend with his wife and kids. There would be plenty to do during the week as the trial progressed.

Gideon spent the rest of the morning polishing his opening statement. He read through again the Allen Henderson piece. It needed virtually no revision. He would begin the opening statement by poking holes into Morgan's case. In the middle, he would chronicle the history of Western Health Corp. to give the jury a sense of the type of reputable company involved. He would contrast Western Health Corp.'s reputation with that of Morgan himself. He would finish the opening statement with his strongest point: Marvil was unquestionably a safe drug, and hence no one at Western Health Corp. could have had any reason to terminate Morgan, even if they had known about his complaints about Marvil.

Gideon rehearsed his opening statement on several occasions. He could not help, however, but have his imagination run a little freely. He was still troubled by Henderson's revelation this morning about his trip Western Health Corp. Why would Henderson go out to Western Health Corp. on his own? He could have easily just called Ted Greene or his secretary and asked for them to send him any promotional material. A sickening thought ran through Gideon's mind. Henderson had said he had gone out there late one evening. He had said it was about three weeks ago. That was right about the time that Alex Benczik was murdered. The police had no suspects. But, Gideon concluded, what possible reason would Henderson have

156

to kill Benczik? It was absurd. He had been working too hard. First, he thought Ali killed Benczik; now he suspected Henderson. He was being irrational. Benczik was a good witness for the company. Why would Ali, who wanted him to succeed in the case, or Henderson, who had similar aspirations, have any reason to kill Alex Benczik?

Gideon was beginning to confuse himself. The last thing he needed to do two days before trial was to worry about such crazy things. But he could not get the coincidences out of his mind. He began to imagine the most sinister things. Perhaps Ali, who had become tired of long nights at home alone, really did not want Gideon to win this case and become a partner. But could she really go to the lengths of purchasing a gun and shooting Gideon's key witness? It simply didn't make sense.

How about Henderson? Did he, deep down, want to see Gideon fail? Maybe Henderson thought that his written work would be noticed, and that Gideon would take the blame for a poor performance at trial. Maybe that would raise Henderson's worth in the eyes of some of the partners, while making Gideon seem less important. Again, Gideon was mad at himself for even thinking such thoughts. Henderson had been nothing but a good friend to him through the years. How could he even imagine such a scenario?

5

"This is a case about corporate greed," Jacobs declared as he faced the jury on the first day of trial. "This defendant, Western Health Corp., cares more about making a buck than about the safety of the public. They manufactured an unsafe drug and hid it from the FDA. My client, Jerry Morgan, discovered this, but before he could go public, he was fired." Gideon tried to show no facial expression during Jacobs, speech. The jury was clearly riveted. If what Jacobs was saying was true, the jury would no doubt return a big verdict for Morgan. Gideon consoled himself with the knowledge that the jury would want Jacobs to back up his word – to prove Marvil was unsafe. If Jacobs could not deliver, the jury would vote in favor of Western Health Corp. Gideon would have to remind the jury of Jacobs' bold statement and turn it against him.

Jacobs' opening statement was well-polished. While not terribly accomplished in writing briefs or taking depositions, Jacobs had a natural and likeable approach before a jury. He was comfortable around the courtroom. He walked to the jury box on several occasions and spoke directly to the jurors. His theme was repetitive. The company wanted to make money at all costs. His client knew that Marvil was unsafe and was fired for attempting to disclose that information. Jacobs said this to the jury in about five different ways during his hour and a half opening statement.

On several occasions, Gideon was inclined to object to certain portions of Jacobs' opening statement when he was clearly becoming argumentative. However, he thought the best course was to sit back and let Jacobs say his piece. He would have his chance to get the jury's attention.

Jacobs had given an emotional well-focused opening statement. At times, Gideon thought, Jacobs had begun to lose the attention of the jury. It is hard to pay attention for such a long period of time. Gideon's tactic in his opening statement would be different: He planned only on going about a half hour in his explanation to the jury. He did not want any lulls in the action, or to lose their attention.

Gideon could sense that Jacobs was about to sum up his case for the jury. After a number of minutes of measured words, Jacobs whirled towards the jury and walked directly up to the jury box. He leaned over so that he was literally in one of the juror's face.

"Ladies and Gentlemen, you have a difficult job in the next several days. I ask your undivided attention to all of the testimony. Assess these witnesses. Listen to what my client has to say. Listen to what the witnesses of the defense have to say. Weigh all the evidence, and most of all, use your common sense. And I am confident that when you hear all the evidence, you'll do justice for my client."

"All right, Ladies and Gentlemen," Judge Farmer bellowed,

"you have just heard the opening statement from the plaintiff's counsel. We will take a 15-minute recess, and you will hear the opening statement from defendant's counsel. Remember, you have not heard any evidence in this case. I ask that you not talk about this case at the break. When you come back, give Mr. Brown your full and undivided attention."

Farmer rose and entered his chambers in the back of the courtroom. The jurors milled out in the hallway. Greene, who was sitting at counsel table, whispered some words of encouragement to Gideon. Gideon went to the hallway to get a drink of water and collect his thoughts.

In the hallway, Gideon was surprised to see the two policemen who were at Western Health Corp. the day Alex Benczik was found murdered. Of all the distractions, Gideon thought to himself. Not only was nearly everyone Gideon knew in the courtroom – Ali, Henderson, McCabe, to name a few – but now the police presence would surely turn the trial into a circus. One of the officers approached Gideon as he turned away from the water fountain. "Mr. Brown, sorry to disturb you during the trial, but we thought you would want to know about our latest lead."

"Officers, of course I am interested, but this really is not a good time. You should not be anywhere near me during the trial. Especially when the jury is out on recess. They should not see you talking to me. Who knows what the jury might think of such circumstances? I suggest you leave immediately and call me at my office at about 5 p.m. after the trial is done for the day. I also am going to have to tell Judge Farmer that you were in the hallway, so that he can declare a mistrial if he thinks this might impact the jury. Now get the hell out of here."

Gideon could not believe he was speaking to the police in such a harsh tone. But it was an awfully stupid decision on the part of the police. They should know better than to appear in the middle of a trial and run the risk of disturbing the proceedings.

Gideon entered the courtroom and asked the bailiff to see the judge in chambers before the jury was called in. Gideon told Jacobs what had occurred in the hallway, and both agreed that it should not have any impact on the trial. They both went back to Farmer's chambers to apprise him of what had occurred.

"Your Honor," Gideon began, "I just wanted to make you aware that during the break, the police who are investigating the Alex Benczik murder came up to me to discuss a lead in that case. I quickly told them that this was not the appropriate place to have such a conversation, but that they should call me later at the office. Of course, if anything they say impacts the fairness of this proceeding, I will alert Your Honor immediately. I do not think any juror saw me, and Mr. Jacobs agrees that we should just go forward. Perhaps, though, Your Honor, you ought to instruct the jury when they come back in that some police officers were in the hallway, but their presence had nothing to do with the case."

"I appreciate your candor and concern, Mr. Brown. I don't

think that's going to be necessary. If I say something, it will just escalate the matter. The jurors may well think that police in the hallway of a courtroom is a normal occurrence. As long as both of you have no objection, I will just let things ride and go directly to your opening statement." Neither Gideon nor Jacobs voiced any disagreement.

As Gideon left the judge's chambers, he could not but wonder what news the police had in store. And, why would they be so anxious to tell him?

6

The jury walked back into the courtroom to take their seat. Several gazed over at Gideon as he awaited Judge Farmer's cue to begin his opening statement. The jury wanted to hear Western Health Corp.'s story.

Gideon knew that he needed to do something early in his opening statement to neutralize the effect of Jacobs' passionate plea. He needed to change the jury's focus from this case being one little man against the big bad corporation. He thus decided to personalize his client by having the jury focus on the man behind Western Health Corp., not the company itself.

Judge Farmer took the bench. "Mr. Brown, you may proceed."

"Ladies and Gentlemen, thank you for your patience. My name is Gideon Brown, and I represent the defendant Western Health Corp. in this case. Seated next to me is Ted Greene, the president of defendant. You will be hearing from Ted during this trial."

Gideon had purposely used Greene's first name in referring to him before the jury. Throughout the trial, he would refer to Jerry Morgan as Mr. Morgan, and all the other witnesses as Mister. But Greene, he wanted the jury to think of as Ted. Juries are must less likely to render big verdicts when they feel some type of personal connection to the defendant.

"Now, during his opening statement, Mr. Jacobs made quite an accusation against Ted Greene and his company. He has told you that Marvil is unsafe. He has promised to prove that to you. Ladies and Gentlemen, Mr. Jacobs has made a promise that he cannot keep. The evidence will show that Marvil is not only completely safe, but that it has revolutionized the treatment of depression in this country. I promise to show you during this case that Marvil was subject to rigorous testing, that the Federal Drug Administration, the government agency responsible for approving all new drugs that come on the market, found that Marvil was completely safe. Your job during this trial is to determine who keeps his promise: Mr. Jacobs or me."

Gideon turned away from the jury and stared into Jacobs eyes. Jacobs was expressionless. The jury was writing notes. Gideon had gotten their attention.

"You see, Mr. Morgan's case makes absolutely no sense unless he can show that Marvil was unsafe. His theory, as I understand it, is that Ted Greene fired him to cover up Mr. Morgan's complaints about the safety of Marvil. Once you see that Marvil was and is completely safe, you will realize that there is nothing to Mr. Morgan's case. And, as the evidence will show, since Mr. Morgan's termination, he has raised his concerns about the safety of Marvil and made it public, yet neither the FDA nor any other medical testing organization has found anything wrong with Marvil."

"Then what possible reason would Morgan have to make these complaints, you might ask yourself? Well, let's put ourselves in Mr. Morgan's shoes for a moment. Mr. Morgan had worked at Western Health Corp. for about 5-1/2 years. It was the best job he ever had. He had a couple of other jobs in the past, one was for a computer company that went bankrupt; the next was as a stockbroker. He left that job because he couldn't cut it. Now he finds himself at Western Health Corp., a growing company, a company which expects its employees to produce."

"But Mr. Morgan didn't cut it at Western Health Corp., either. The evidence will show that as a sales representative, his productivity the year before he was terminated was the worst of all of the sales reps. The evidence will show that Mr. Morgan was warned about this by the company in writing. The evidence will also show that Mr. Morgan's reaction to this was not to improve his productivity, but to be absent more frequently and to refuse Ted Greene's efforts to assist him in his performance. Rather than blaming himself, Ladies and Gentlemen, Mr. Morgan has done something very common: he's blaming someone else. You are to judge for yourself during this trial who is really to blame."

Gideon walked away from the jury and back to counsel table. He paused both for effect and to gather his thoughts. He took a sip of water and glanced at Greene. Greene gave Gideon a comforting nod of approval. Gideon then moved away from such generalities to the specifics of the case. He explained to the jury in detail Western Health Corp.'s history. He explained what a biotechnology company like Western Health Corp. does. It was important for the jury to know that Western Health Corp.'s business involved creating new drugs which could help fight the country's worst diseases. He told the jury that Western Health Corp. was in the process of trying to develop a drug which would help fight the HIV virus.

He explained to the jury the process by which a drug developed by Western Health Corp. gets approval to be sold to the public. Western Health Corp. itself does not decide to sell the drug to the public, Gideon explained. A government agency, the FDA, had the final say on that. When a company like Western Health Corp. develops a drug which it believes is safe for public consumption, at that point the FDA is called in and does their own thorough investigation. That is precisely what happened in this case, Gideon told the jury.

Gideon advised the jury that Western Health Corp.'s chief chemist had been in charge of developing the drug from the start. He would not be able to testify, Gideon declared, because he had unfortunately passed away. However, the jury would have the benefit of hearing Benczik's testimony from his deposition read during the course of the trial. They were to listen carefully to the testimony and give it the same weight as if it had been through live testimony. Gideon told the jury that the judge would so instruct them.

"And when you get done listening to Mr. Benczik's testimony, and when you get done listening to Ted Greene's testimony, I am confident that you will have no doubt that Marvil is completely safe. Even so, you may be asking yourself the question, why couldn't Jerry Morgan cut it at Western Health Corp.? I mean, he appears to a bright, energetic individual."

Gideon turned and pointed to Morgan, who was sitting a counsel table next to Jacobs. "He liked his job, didn't want to work elsewhere. Well, we don't know exactly why Jerry Morgan did not work out at Western Health Corp. But we have some clues. The evidence will show that Mr. Morgan was arrested for drug use back in the late 1970s. He was institutionalized. After his job with the stockbrokerage house didn't work out, he was again institutionalized."

"Mr. Morgan is going to get up to testify before you and is going to be unable to explain either his arrest or the times he was institutionalized. He is going to tell you he simply doesn't remember it. Now I'm not going to stand here and accuse Mr. Morgan of using drugs at Western Health Corp. We have no evidence of that; we do not claim that he did. But what we do know is that there have been periods in Mr. Morgan's life where he has had difficulty coping. And, the evidence will show, that in the six months prior to his termination, Mr. Morgan was absent so frequently that his productivity became the worst of all marketing employees at Western Health Corp."

"Now, Western Health Corp. certainly didn't fire Jerry

Morgan because he was absent and couldn't cope. In fact, the evidence will show that Ted Greene had a personal meeting with Mr. Morgan to talk about his situation. Ted offered Mr. Morgan the opportunity to take part in Western Health Corp.'s employee assistance program. That is a program which any employee can use, free of charge, on a totally confidential basis, when they have any personal problems of any sort. Mr. Morgan refused. Mr. Morgan told Ted Greene that he had no problems, that it was none of Ted Greene's business. You see, Mr. Morgan was wrong. It is Ted Greene's business if an employee isn't doing his job. That is why Western Health Corp. has the reputation in the United States that it does. That is why Ted Greene had to make the difficult choice to terminate Mr. Morgan."

Gideon knew that the fact that Morgan had a past history of drug use would not alone in the jury's mind justify his termination. He tried to make it clear that Ted Greene and Western Health Corp. were sympathetic to Mr. Morgan's problems, but that Morgan would not even attempt to change his ways. He thought that the jury would approve of a termination under the circumstances.

Gideon had spoken to the jury for close to a half hour. He wanted to wrap up on a strong point.

"Mr. Jacobs and I are going to disagree about a lot during this trial. But there is one thing we do agree about. We both want you to sit back and weigh all the evidence. We both want you to do what is fair. And all I ask as you weigh the evidence, is to remember what

I told you in the beginning of my opening statement. There have been two promises made to you. One by Mr. Jacobs. One by me. As you listen to the witnesses, as you listen to Mr. Morgan, as you listen to Ted Greene, think to yourself, who has kept their promise. Thank you."

7

Judge Farmer told the jury that they would recess for a long lunch and be expected to be back by 1:30 p.m. Gideon decided to go back to the office for the break.

When he returned to the office, there was a message waiting from the police officer. Gideon called the number immediately. He got Sgt. Delaney on the line. "Mr. Brown, sorry about the mix up this morning, but I thought you would want to know as soon as we had a lead in the case. It turns out that on the day Alex Benczik was murdered, he made several telephone calls. One of the telephone calls was to a fellow named Jerry Morgan, who I understand is the plaintiff in your case. We, of course, don't know what the telephone conversation was about, but it strikes me as kind of odd that there would be a telephone call between a company witness and the plaintiff. Do you know anything about it?"

Gideon was stunned. He did not know anything about it. He had admonished Benczik and all the other Western Health Corp. employees to not have any conversations with either the plaintiff or his counsel. Benczik seemed the least likely to ignore that admonition. His whole life had been spent going by the book, so to speak.

"I had never heard about this phone call," Gideon told Sgt.

Delaney. "It does seem very strange. I advise all my clients not to speak to the other side outside my presence. What do you make of this, Sergeant?"

Sgt. Delaney said that he thought the telephone call was not a coincidence. He, too, thought it would be strange that Benczik would telephone Morgan. But perhaps Morgan had called Benczik at work and tried to reach him. Perhaps Morgan had left a message or a note to Benczik, and Benczik was just extending the courtesy of returning a call to a former employee. "Whatever the explanation," Sgt. Delaney said, "we think it is awfully suspicious. This has to make Jerry Morgan our number one suspect."

8

Gideon had told Sgt. Delaney that, because the conversation between Morgan and Benczik might have an impact on the current trial, he felt obligated to talk to Morgan's lawyer Jacobs about it. Sgt. Delaney had no problem with that. He intended to question Morgan after the trial. He felt that any action by the police during the trial could taint the proceedings.

Gideon raced back to the courtroom and sought out Jacobs. Jacobs was sitting on a bench outside the courtroom next to Morgan. Gideon approached. "Listen, Bill, I need a word with you alone, if we could." Jacobs and Gideon walked together down the hallway. "If you're going to make a settlement offer," Jacobs said to Gideon, "forget it. My client's just not interested. We've gotten this far, and he wants to tell his story." "That's not what I have in mind, Bill, not at all. I've got to ask you something, and I need a straight answer. Sgt. Delaney of the L.A.P.D. gave me a call today at lunch at the office. He says that on the day of Alex Benczik's murder, there was a phone call placed from Benczik to Morgan. I'm obviously going to let the police do their own investigation, but I am very concerned about what that means to this case. You're well aware, I'm sure, that any contact between your client and Mr. Benczik should have been revealed."

"Gideon, I have no knowledge at all about this telephone call. I'll talk to Morgan right away and find out what the conversation was about. If it has anything to do with this case, I'll tell you and divulge it to Judge Farmer. It's not my intent to have anything underhanded going on here."

Gideon remained in place as Jacobs ambled back down the hallway to talk to Morgan. The two exchanged words for about three minutes. Jacobs then walked his way back toward Gideon.

"Gideon, I can assure you that nothing was divulged about this case. My client tells me that he received a telephone call from Benczik at about 5:00 p.m. on that day. He was very surprised to hear from Benczik. Before Benczik could say anything, he was interrupted. He told Morgan that he would call back later. He never did."

With that assurance, Gideon felt that the phone call had no impact on the case. He chatted with Jacobs and urged Jacobs to have Morgan call the police with the information at the end of the day, so that the police could continue their investigation. Jacobs vowed to cooperate with the police, and promised Gideon that he would keep him informed if there were any other developments.

The two returned to the courtroom. Judge Farmer was uncharacteristically late taking the bench. At 2:00 p.m., the bailiff finally called the court to order. Judge Farmer took the bench and spoke to counsel outside the presence of the jury.

"Mr. Jacobs and Mr. Brown, I have just been on the phone with Sgt. Delaney of the L.A.P.D. He tells me that their investigation into the death of Alex Benczik has taken a turn. He's discovered that Mr. Benczik placed a call to Mr. Morgan on the day of his death. The L.A.P.D. now considers Morgan a prime suspect. Although I have strong reservations having this trial go forward at this time, I firmly believe that a man is innocent until proven guilty. I do not want to deprive Mr. Morgan of his day in court through a continuance. However, I also do not want to go through an entire trial and then have this issue raised on appeal by either of you. Therefore, I am going to suspend the proceedings today and tomorrow. I want both of you to go back to your office and research this issue. I want written briefs in my courtroom at 9:00 a.m. on Wednesday on the issue of whether I should call a mistrial. I will read your briefs and make my ruling."

Gideon could have kicked himself. He had been so intent on pursuing the trial and winning the case for Western Health Corp., that he neglected to think of the obvious. It may well be that there was some authority out there for the proposition that a civil proceeding could not go forward while criminal charges were possibly going to be brought against one of the parties. He hoped that Greene would not take umbrage at Gideon's oversight.

As they walked back to the office, Gideon was shocked by Greene's response. Far from taking Gideon to task about his oversight, Greene's reaction to Judge Farmer's request was puzzling.

"Gideon, I wouldn't spend too much time on this issue. I think we should take the position in our brief to Judge Farmer that no mistrial is in order here. I am just sick and tired of this case, and now that we are here, let's get it done. Even if the law favors a mistrial, if Jacobs agrees not to raise it on appeal, I think we should waive the argument."

Greene was the client, and what the client says goes. But Gideon felt that he needed to at least discuss the issue with Greene.

"I hear you, Ted, I honestly do. But I want to explore this issue with you just for a minute. Suppose that we do find authority for the judge to call a mistrial. It'll take at least six months to get back on the trial calendar. Within that time, the police may finish its investigation, and it may well lead to charges brought against Morgan. If that is the case, this whole case will go away."

"I'm well aware of that, Gideon, and I know you're just doing your job by informing me of all my options. And I'm making an informed choice. Even if the police do bring charges against Morgan and this case is dropped, there will then be lingering doubts about Western Health Corp.'s innocence. Only a jury's verdict will quell the public's doubts."

As they returned to the office, Gideon told Greene that he would research the issue, and would call him tomorrow with the results of the cases. If what Greene wanted to do was waive the argument, they would certainly do so in the brief. Gideon made it clear, however, that they ought to find out the answer one way or the other so that Judge Farmer would not be angry at them during the remainder of the trial for not thoroughly researching the issue. Greene agreed with Gideon's point.

Gideon went upstairs and headed straight to McCabe's office. He knew McCabe should have the final say on this issue. It cut against Gideon's grain to forego an argument which could well lead to the case being dropped. He wanted the approval of the partner in charge of the case on such a tactical decision.

Gideon bolted to McCabe's office and motioned to him that it was urgent. McCabe finished up a phone call and asked Gideon what was going on. Gideon explained the issue to McCabe in full detail.

"Look, Gideon, I agree with you that as a matter of legal strategy Greene is making a mistake. But he's the client. He pays our bills. Just make sure you make note of his instructions and put it in the file. I have no problem waiving the argument if that's what Greene wants to do."

Gideon left the office and walked back to his, disenchanted. He thought that this was a terrible mistake. Though he was confident about how the opening statement had gone, he thought it was a grave error in not taking advantage of a possible windfall. He found Greene's reaction particularly odd. If Morgan was charged with a crime, and the case dropped, why would anyone conceivably give any credence to Morgan's claim? Wouldn't the case being dropped vindicate Western Health Corp. as much as a jury verdict? The whole thing did not make sense to Gideon.

McCabe's reaction was predictable. He had heard the "client knows best" mantra a million times at Longworth & Drucker. He did not think that McCabe would cross Greene at this point in the game. He wanted Greene's business.

Gideon summoned Henderson to his office and assigned him the job of researching the issue Judge Farmer had asked the parties to brief. Gideon was exhausted, even though the day was still young. The opening statement had sapped his energy. He had given it his all. While he hated to impose on Henderson to research into the night, he knew that Henderson would be way more effective at the task than Gideon could be at this point. He was planning to go home, when one thought crossed his mind. Sgt. Delaney, in the conversation earlier, had mentioned that Benczik had made several phone calls on that day. Shouldn't Gideon find out who else the phone calls were made to? He was not trying to play amateur detective, but he just wanted to make sure that the other calls somehow did not have an impact on the case.

Gideon telephoned Sgt. Delaney, who was quite cooperative. "Yeah," Sgt. Delaney muttered, "I should have told you this before. Benczik made three other phone calls that afternoon, all in rapid succession. The first was to Morgan. The second was to your home phone. I assume he spoke to you that afternoon. The third was to Bart McCabe's number at Longworth & Drucker. I guess maybe he wanted McCabe's opinion about something on the case as well."

Gideon kept silent as he heard this news. There was no way

that Gideon was home at 5:00 p.m., the day of Benczik's murder. It was right before trial, and he was busting his rear-end every day and working until late in the evening. Who the hell had Benczik talked to? Ali? She probably would have been home at 5:00 p.m. on a Thursday, she had the afternoon off on that day.

And why had Benczik called McCabe? McCabe had literally no interaction with Benczik whatsoever during the case. He had remained in touch with Ted Greene, but to Gideon's knowledge, Benczik had never met McCabe nor had any discussions with him. There was something going on that Gideon did not know.

9

Gideon decided that he had waited long enough to confront Ali about his discovery of the handgun, and the telephone call with Alex Benczik. There had to be some credible explanation. He knew that Ali was not a murderer, and there must be some reason why she did not mention Benczik's phone call to her that afternoon. It was time to find out.

Gideon wanted to get home quickly. Of course, leaving the office at 5:00 o'clock, he was mired in Los Angeles rush hour traffic. The freeway was near a standstill. He popped in his Springsteen tape to try to get his mind off everything. It did not help much.

When Gideon finally arrived home, he was seething. It wasn't like Ali to keep secrets from him. He had to get to the bottom of this.

Ali was home, starting dinner. Gideon wasted no time launching into the issue. "Ali, I've got to talk to you about something, it's been bothering me for quite a while."

Ali put down the saucepan and walked with Gideon to the living room. "What's going on, Gideon, you look pale. Did the case go okay this afternoon?"

"Nothing happened this afternoon after you left, Ali. We took a long lunch recess. Then the judge came back and told us to take the afternoon and tomorrow off. There has been a breakthrough in the murder investigation of Alex Benczik. There is some indication that Morgan may be the prime suspect."

"Really," Ali exclaimed, "I can't believe that. I would think someone at Western Health Corp. would have wanted to knock off Benczik sooner than Morgan."

"What do you mean?" Gideon shouted. "That's an incredible statement. What do you mean?"

"Calm down, Gideon, I've been meaning to tell you. You've been so wrapped up in this case that I didn't want to tell you. The day that Alex Benczik was murdered, he called here at the house. I thought it was odd. I'm sure he knew that you were working at the office. It seemed like he wanted to talk to me. He wasn't very coherent. He said that he was having second thoughts about testifying. That he was nervous about being the so-called star witness. That he thought he might crack on the stand. I told him you were at the office, and that he should call you. I told him that you would reassure him. I assumed that he called you, but evidently he didn't."

"Ali, I can't believe that you didn't call me to tell me that a witness in my case spoke to you at home. No, I never did hear from Benczik regarding that. I can't imagine what he had to be nervous about. He was great in his deposition."

"All he had to do was give the same testimony."

"Unless he had something to hide," Ali said. "Benczik didn't sound to me like a confident or willing witness. I'm not meaning to jump to conclusions, but he sounded like a man who needed to get something off his chest. Maybe he didn't tell you everything, Gideon."

Gideon was getting a little angry with Ali's armchair psychiatry. It wasn't all that unusual for witnesses to get cold feet before trial, even though they had given prior deposition testimony. Gideon thought that Ali was misconstruing Benczik's stage fright for misgivings about testifying in court.

"Well, Ali, while we're on the subject of things you haven't told me, there is something else. What in God's earth are you doing with a handgun in this house?"

Ali turned beet red. "How do you know about my handgun?" Ali shot back. "Have you been going through my drawers?"

"No, I have not been going through your drawers. I do write the bills. And I was up late the other night, and restless, and decided to write some bills. You keep them in your drawer. I went to get them, and I found the gun."

"Look, Gideon, you've been out of the house so much recently and have been getting home so late, that I wanted some protection. I've been beside myself. I mean, I know that nothing is going to happen, but I just feel safer with a gun in the house."

Gideon was thankful there was some rational explanation for the gun. He didn't feel it wise or necessary to delve any further into the coincidence that Benczik had been killed with a 45-shotgun revolver the night he called Gideon at home and spoke to Ali. The phone call to Ali had been about 5:15 p.m. Gideon tried to think back as to what time he got home that night. He thought it was probably about 9:00 p.m. Ali was home when he got home at 9:00 p.m. that night. Western Health Corp. was a good hour away without traffic, an hour and a half with. It was possible that Ali could have gone out there and back and been home by 9:00 p.m., but unlikely.

Gideon decided not to let his imagination run wild. Ali was not the killing type. She was not as intent, obviously, on winning the case as Gideon. He decided to drop the issue. He needed some rest.

10

Gideon was eager to get back to the courtroom and continue the trial. He needed to put all these distractions aside. His number one priority was winning the case for Western Health Corp. He knew that in order to do so he would have to do an effective cross-examination of Morgan.

Not surprisingly, Morgan was to be Jacobs' first witness. Gideon would not be surprised if he was the only witness. But first Judge Farmer would want to meet with the lawyers in chambers to see what, if anything, needed to be done about the Benczik murder investigation and the mistrial issue.

Henderson's research disclosed nothing which would require Judge Farmer to call a mistrial; this pleased Greene. Gideon was relieved to learn that Jacobs had similarly found no authority on the issue. It was therefore quite likely that Judge Farmer would allow the trial to proceed on schedule.

Judge Farmer was in a jovial mood when he called Gideon and Jacobs into chambers. "I am proud to say that this is the only civil case I have ever heard of in which a murder investigation was proceeding during the trial. There certainly does not appear to be any authority on this issue one way or another. I thank you both for

183

researching this and giving me your conclusions. It appears that all of us agree that the trial should go forward at this time and that no mistrial is requested."

"That is certainly our position, your Honor," Gideon responded. "In fact, my client has authorized me to state on the record that Western Health Corp will not raise this issue on any appeal of this case."

"My client has given me similar authority, your Honor," Jacobs pitched in. "I think we have a stipulation that the case should proceed."

"Very well," Judge given Farmer replied, "I see no reason, given the position of the parties, to call a mistrial. Let us conduct the remainder of this case as if nothing had happened. I fully expect that neither of you will mention the murder investigation in front of the jury. Now we'll go back to the business at hand. The bailiff will call in the jury, and Mr. Jacobs, you will call your first witness. I'll see both of you in the courtroom in ten minutes." Judge Farmer led the two out of his chambers and motioned the bailiff to summon the jury. The trial would finally proceed.

Gideon and Jacobs had a moment to chat in the hallway before the trial resumed. The two gave each other an estimate of the time each planned to take with their witnesses. As Gideon had expected, Jacobs only planned to call Morgan during his case in chief before resting, although he reserved the right to call additional witnesses during rebuttal, if necessary. Gideon advised Jacobs that he planned to read portions of Benczik's deposition testimony, then call Williams, then conclude with Greene. There would be no surprises, or so Gideon thought. The trial would probably last a week at most before the jury would be allowed to deliberate.

11

If Jack Morgan had his way, he would throw a wrinkle into the orderly trial planned by Gideon and Jacobs. Jack's operative, Gonzales, was finally paying dividends. He had gained the confidence of several Western Health Corp. employees and had learned some interesting information. Apparently, all was not perfect at the company. Several employees had confided to Gonzales that things were quite tense at Western Health Corp. during the Marvil approval process. Morgan had not been the only person to have heard words exchanged between Benczik and Greene. In fact, the two had yelled at each other more than once during the process.

In addition, Gonzales had learned that Benczik, shortly before his murder, had threatened to resign. Unfortunately, none of the employees knew what had precipitated Benczik's ultimatum. The only thing they knew was that after a lengthy closed-door meeting between Benczik and Greene, Benczik had decided to stay with the company. Benczik had simply never confided to anyone the reason for his disagreement with Greene.

Jack Morgan desperately wanted this information to come out in front of the jury. While it did not directly implicate anyone other than his son in Benczik's death, it certainly would bolster his son's theory that Greene and Benczik were arguing over the safety of Marvil, and that his son was fired for fear that he had overheard something damaging to Western Health Corp.

Jack Morgan would not have a chance to catch Jacobs before the trial began. He would have to communicate this information to Jacobs during a break. Of course, he knew that Jacobs would be displeased that he had taken matters into his own hands. But Jacobs would be hard pressed to argue with the result. He would finally be able to present evidence to support Jerry Morgan's theory.

Jack Morgan got down to the courthouse just as Jacobs was putting his son on the witness stand. Jerry Morgan had finally listened to Jacobs. He was in a new suit, not too flashy, and looked dignified. His hair was neatly trimmed. He had an air of confidence. He looked directly at the jury as Jacobs began to pose his questions.

Jacobs started the questioning in dramatic fashion. "Mr. Morgan, would you tell this jury why you are here today in this courtroom?"

Morgan eyed the jury and responded in a measured yet stirring manner. "I believe that I was fired from Western Health Corp. because Ted Greene was afraid that I had learned damaging information about the safety of a drug called Marvil. I believe, in fact, that Marvil is not a safe drug. I come to this courtroom to expose the dangers of Marvil before it is too late."

Gideon sat back and took notes of Morgan's answer. While Jacobs had started the trial effectively, Gideon knew that he could turn this testimony against Morgan during cross-examination and in his closing argument. The answer fit in well with the theme he had established during his opening statement – that Jacobs and Morgan would make promises that could not be kept. In this instance, Gideon would emphasize that Morgan simply had no proof that Marvil was unsafe, and that he was making a wild and unfounded accusation. He would try to convince the jury that Morgan was simply trying to blame others for his woes, when the blame belonged on him.

Jacobs then shifted gears and had Morgan provide the jury with his educational and employment background. Morgan answered the questions directly and with conviction. Gideon began, for the first time, to worry about how the trial was going. He could tell that the jury was being attentive and liked Morgan so far. The picture Jacobs was painting for the jury was that Morgan, a well-educated young man, had worked his way up the corporate ladder until he received the job of his dreams – a marketing position at Western Health Corp. In fact, Morgan testified that his goal, before being fired, was to work his way into an executive position at Western Health Corp.

Gideon wondered whether Jacobs would allude on direct examination to Morgan's troubled past. Gideon thought it would be a grave error on Jacobs' part to completely ignore the issue. The conventional wisdom among trial lawyers is that it is important during direct examination to attempt to diffuse any bad facts that might be raised in cross-examination. Jacobs decided to address the issue with Morgan. "Now, Mr. Morgan, we heard Mr. Brown say in his opening statement that you were arrested back in the 1980's on some drug charges. Is that in fact true, Mr. Morgan?"

A. "Yes sir, it is true," Morgan responded, without even an ounce of shame.

Q. "When was the last time that you used drugs, Jerry?"

A. "I've been clean since the day that I started at Western Health Corp."

Q. "Are you absolutely sure?" Jacobs asked.

A. "Yes sir, I am."

Gideon was absolutely livid. He knew that Morgan was lying through his teeth. And he couldn't believe that Jacobs would have the gall to elicit such testimony. It was close to suborning perjury.

Henderson was sitting at counsel table, next to Gideon, assisting on the trial. Gideon wrote a note on a yellow sheet of paper. He was blunt. "Call the fucking P.I. Tell him we need to nail the son of a bitch on drug use since 1986."

"Give him 24 hours. Money is no object."

12

There was more activity out of the trial than in the trial during the remainder of the day. Jacobs spent a lot of time questioning Morgan about his job duties at Western Health Corp. He went into painstaking detail regarding the day-to-day responsibilities of Morgan. He was trying to impress the jury with the amount of things Morgan did on a daily basis, in order to counter the information Jacobs knew would come out on cross and during the direct examination of Western Health Corp. witnesses about Morgan's alleged lack of productivity.

Meanwhile, Gideon's P.I. was scrambling for information. He had previously determined that Morgan had no arrest record since 1979. He also knew that Morgan was last institutionalized in 1986. He would have to learn about Morgan through other means.

Jack Morgan was in the back of the courtroom enjoying his son's testimony and Jacobs' performance. Although he had doubted Jacobs' resolve during the litigation, Jacobs seemed quite at home in the courtroom. He was giving it his all. Jack Morgan felt that the additional information he had learned from Gonzales might break the case open. He wanted to share his discovery with Jacobs at the first convenient moment. But because Jacobs had such momentum going, he decided to wait until the end of the day. He did not want to upset Jacobs during his direct examination of his son.

The P.I. knew only one sure fire way to get information about Morgan on such an expedited basis. He would not tell Gideon about the method he would employ. Then again, Gideon never asked.

The P.I. went to Morgan's apartment. He got into the building with no problem. He approached Morgan's door and looked around to make sure nobody was around. There was no one in sight. The P.I. eyed a window near the kitchen.

He took out an electric drill from his coat pocket and quickly bore a hole through the bottom of the windowsill. He then took out a long screwdriver and put it through the hole he had just drilled. He pressed down hard on the screwdriver and jimmied up the window. Despite the fact that it was locked, he was able to apply enough pressure to the window to pop the lock and pry the window open. He crawled through the window and shut it behind him.

Morgan would never know that his apartment had been entered.

The P.I. glanced through the apartment, trying to find something. The apartment was a mess. Morgan's clothes were strewn on the floor. He opened Morgan's drawers. At the bottom of the sock drawer he found a razor blade. Next to it was a vial filled with a white powdery substance. It was cocaine.

The P.I. knew that he could not confiscate the cocaine. Gideon would throw a shit-fit. It was not admissible in court.

Locating the cocaine, however, strengthened the P.I.'s resolve. He knew that there must be something in the apartment that would nail Morgan.

He spied an ashtray on the coffee table. Next to it was a book of matches. The P.I. recognized the name on the matches immediately. It was from the strip joint by the airport. A wild place. The P.I. had been there himself on several occasions.

He took the matches and put them in his pocket. He would go there immediately. He needed a picture of Morgan to show around the joint. He located a photograph album. There was a picture of Morgan at his parents' house. It looked pretty recent. The P.I. grabbed the photo and headed straight to the airport.

13

The direct examination of Morgan took an entire day. At about 3:45 p.m., Jacobs began to bring the testimony to a conclusion. He saved his best for last.

"Mr. Morgan, they claim you were unproductive before you were fired. Is that true?"

"That is not true. I admit, things were slow, but it wasn't my fault. They gave me the worst clients. So, naturally, my productivity did not look good on paper. But, I swear, I continued to try as hard as I did when I first started at Western Health Corp., and they never had any problems with me then."

"How about the absenteeism, Jerry?"

"Sure, I was absent a bit too much. But that was because I had nothing to do. They wanted me to call the same clients over and over again, the same ones who repeatedly told me that they were not interested in Western Health Corp. products. There was no sense coming in all of the time, unless they gave me some new clients."

"Why do you think that they didn't give you any new clients?"

Gideon rose to his feet. This was a crucial part of the case, and he thought the question was objectionable. It was time to give a little speech to the jury.

"Your Honor," Gideon implored, "that question calls for pure conjecture and speculation on the part of this witness. We've sat through a full day of testimony, and Mr. Jacobs has not introduced a shred of evidence to show any improper motive on the part of my client. I strongly object." "I tend to agree Mr. Jacobs," Judge Farmer responded. "I've given you a lot of latitude here, and so has Mr. Brown. I don't want to hear Mr. Morgan's opinion. It is speculative. It is not relevant. You need to lay some foundation. Objection sustained."

"Your Honor, I will lay the foundation," Jacobs responded, showing no emotion to the jury. "Mr. Morgan, you were fired on what day?"

"Friday the 13th, I guess it was an unlucky day for me."

"Did anything happen shortly before that day that leads you to believe that there was something fishy about your termination?"

Gideon rose to his feet again. "I have to object again, your Honor. The question is argumentative. It assumes facts not in evidence. It asks for this witness's lay opinion, which is not relevant."

"Objection sustained. Mr. Jacobs, just ask Mr. Morgan what happened in the workplace prior to the time he was fired. That is admissible, although it may not be all that probative."

Gideon was pleased with Judge Farmer's response. He was telling the jury in a subtle way that Jacobs had not made out much of a case. He was also giving the jury a hint as to how he viewed the testimony he knew Jacobs was about to elicit. While a judge is technically not supposed to comment at all about the evidence that is presented in the courtroom, it is quite common for judges to speak freely to the lawyers in front of the jury, sometimes to the dismay of the attorneys who are trying the case. In this circumstance, Gideon, as the beneficiary of Judge Farmer's remarks, thought that Judge Farmer was only following up on his warning to Jacobs during the earlier hearing – that he needed to present more than the slim evidence of the conversation he overheard in order to prevail in the case.

Jacobs, though rebuked, continued on with his questioning. "Mr. Morgan, what happened in the workplace prior to your termination?"

A. "I overheard a conversation, a loud conversation, in Ted Greene's office."

Q. "How soon was that prior to your termination?"

A. "It was about two weeks prior to my termination."

Q. "What was said?"

A. "I heard Ted Greene shouting. I don't know who else was in his office. But I did hear Marvil mentioned. Then I heard Greene say that he had discussed the matter enough, that the person with him knew what had to be done. I kept walking, but I heard the door fling open. I'm sure that they saw me and that's why they fired me."

"Your Honor," Gideon said as he rose to his feet. "I move to strike the last sentence of Mr. Morgan's response and ask that the jury be admonished to disregard it. It is quite proper for Mr. Morgan to testify about what he claims he heard. It is another thing, however, for Mr. Morgan to speculate that Greene or anyone else fired him because of his overhearing a completely innocent conversation between two people who were working night and day and who were under a lot of stress. The jury is to decide whether there was anything improper about Mr. Morgan's termination."

Judge Farmer stated, "Motion to strike is granted. Ladies and gentlemen of the jury, you are to disregard Mr. Morgan's statement that he was fired because he overheard the conversation in Greene's office. That is not admissible evidence. The only evidence you have before you is that this conversation took place, that Morgan overheard it, and that Greene was aware that Morgan overheard it. That is the only admissible evidence from Mr. Morgan's testimony. Your job is to decide, after hearing all of the evidence, including Mr. Greene's testimony, whether Morgan was fired because of his overhearing this conversation about Marvil and further, whether this conversation provides evidence that Marvil was unsafe and that Greene knew that Morgan thought Marvil was unsafe. I will instruct you later on this in greater detail before you deliberate. Now, Mr. Jacobs, you may proceed."

Q. "Mr. Morgan, why do you think that Marvil is unsafe?"

A. "The drug was approved faster than any drug I had ever heard of. That struck me as unusual. Then I overheard the conversation about Marvil in Ted Greene's office. Then I was fired. When you put all of that together, that is why I think that there is something wrong with Marvil."

"Thank you, Mr. Morgan, that's all I have."

Judge Farmer concluded, "All right, ladies and gentlemen, it is nearly 4:00 p.m. We are through for the day. You are not to discuss this case among yourselves. You are to keep an open mind until you hear all of the evidence. Please be here at 9:00 a.m. tomorrow morning, at which point Mr. Brown will conduct his cross-examination of Mr. Morgan. Good day."

The jury was led out of the courtroom by the bailiff. Gideon sat at the counsel table and spoke with Greene about the day's events. Both felt that Judge Farmer had kept close control of the trial. Both thought that his comments in front of the jury were helpful. Both were anxiously awaiting the cross-examination of Morgan.

Jack Morgan could barely contain himself while Jacobs and his son walked out of the courtroom. He had thought that the beginning of the testimony went well, but he clearly believed that Judge Farmer was against Jerry and was making his feelings known to the jury. He now felt, more than ever, that additional testimony on his son's behalf was critical.

"Bill, good job today, although it looks like we have a tough judge. I've got some news. What if I told you that there are some Western Health Corp. employees who are willing to corroborate Jerry's testimony? What if I told you that they will testify that they also overheard arguments between Greene and Benczik? Wouldn't that help our case?"

"Of course, it would, Jack, but how in the hell did you discover this information? You know, there are ways to go about that in discovery, but our discovery disclosed nothing."

"I don't have to tell you Bill, you're not my lawyer. Just suppose these employees are willing to meet you in your office at 7:00 p.m. tonight. You can listen to what they have to say. You can decide whether it is worth calling them as witnesses."

"Well, Jack, I think the other side will object to our calling them as witnesses, but we can try. At this point, I agree, we need to pull out all the stops to try to win this case. I'll talk to them."

14

The P.I. spent the afternoon at the strip joint at the airport. He showed the picture of Morgan to all the patrons as well as the bartender. The patrons were of no help. But the bartender thought that he recognized Morgan. He told the P.I. to wait until the girls on the night shift arrived. He would show the picture to the girls for $100. The P.I. slipped him a $100 bill and told him to tell the girls there was $200 for anyone who could give him some useful information.

Angel arrived at 7:00 p.m. The bartender cornered her before she changed into her outfit. Angel was a businesswoman. She was ready and willing to talk to the P.I.

"Do you recognize this guy?" the P.I. asked. "If you do, there's a lot more where this came from," he said, holding two crisp $100 bills.

"Yeah, I recognize him, he comes in now and then. One time, he gave me a $20 bill when I was dancing and asked me if I wanted to snort some coke. You're not a cop, are you? You're not going to try to bust me over this, because I'll deny everything!"

"I assure you, I'm not a cop, and I'm not going to try to bust you."

"Well, as I was saying, he offered me some blow, and I wanted to get high, so I did some lines with him in his car. We had sex at his place. What else do you want to know?"

"That's quite enough, Angel, listen, tell me how much you make in an evening here and I'll pay you double. I want you to meet someone. I'll clear it with your boss."

The P.I. slipped the proprietor of the strip joint a $100 bill and asked that Angel be given the night off. The proprietor readily agreed. Angel and the P.I. drove immediately downtown to the office of Longworth & Drucker, where Gideon was working late into the night preparing for his cross-examination.

Angel and the P.I. told Gideon the story. Gideon could hardly contain himself. "We have quite a surprise in store for Mr. Morgan tomorrow morning. Angel, honey, all you have to do is walk into the courtroom when my colleague Allen Henderson tells you. Just sit in the back. You'll never have to testify. The P.I. will make sure that you're well paid."

15

Gideon got home at about 10:00 p.m. after his meeting with Angel. Ali had been in the courtroom to observe the day's events, but of course knew nothing about the surprise appearance of Angel set for the next morning. Since Gideon knew that Ali planned to be in court again in the morning, he decided to tell Ali about his new trial strategy.

Ali was awake when Gideon drove into the garage. She greeted him outside and gave him a kiss as he walked through the back door. "Long day, Gideon, you should get some rest before your cross of Morgan."

"I'm so pumped up I don't think I'll get much sleep. But I have an ace up my sleeve for tomorrow morning." "What do you mean by that?" Ali inquired. "I thought you said there would be no real surprises, since everybody's deposition had been taken."

"Well, do you remember this morning when Morgan gave that bullshit testimony about how he's been clean since the day he started at Western Health Corp? I had the P.I. nose around a bit. And he found out that good old Jerry Morgan has been up to his old tricks. I'm going to scare the pants off of Jerry by having this hooker with whom he snorted coke in the back of the courtroom. Of course, I'll never call her to testify, the jury would hate her. But I'll bet Jerry will confess all and the jury will know that he is a lying sack of shit."

Ali was appalled by Gideon's cavalier attitude toward destroying Morgan. She felt that he had begun to personalize this case and as the trial came closer and closer, became more aggressive and vindictive toward Morgan.

"I don't see what in God's earth Morgan's snorting coke has to do with this lawsuit. I mean, you already told the jury about his past drug use. He's already admitted to it. Yeah, maybe he told a little white lie today, but you don't have to destroy him, Gideon. The jury's going to know that he just suddenly didn't stop using drugs, not when he was involved with a drug like PCP."

Gideon was annoyed by Ali's knee jerk reaction. "Ali, for Christ sake, he lied through his teeth today. He's trying to make the jury feel sorry for him. I can't take any chances. He could have played it straight, but he didn't. The gloves are off. This is trial, no holds barred."

"You're really letting them change you. What happened to Gideon the liberal, Gideon the ethical lawyer, who would never stoop to such underhanded tactics? I mean, bringing a hooker in a court-room? That's what sleazy personal injury or divorce attorneys would do. I thought Longworth & Drucker was above all that."

After six years at Longworth & Drucker, Gideon was good at rationalization. He firmly believed that the trial could go into the gutter because Morgan was the first to break the rules. He knew that McCabe would back him up on this one. He had the perfect opportunity to impeach a witness, and he simply couldn't give up the chance.

"Look, Ali, I don't need this right now. I've got a busy day tomorrow and I don't want to discuss this anymore. I've got to do anything to win this case; my first allegiance is to my client, Western Health Corp. And if Jerry Morgan goes down, so be it."

16

Gideon got to the courtroom a half hour early. He met the P.I. and Angel in the cafeteria. The plan was simple. They would wait outside while the jury and everyone else went into the courtroom. When the judge took the bench and told Gideon to proceed with his cross-examination, Henderson would get up from counsel table and walk to the back door of the courtroom. As soon as Henderson opened the door, it was Angel's cue to walk into the courtroom and sit in the back row. Gideon would take care of the rest.

Henderson was beginning to have his doubts about the theatrics that Gideon had planned. "Gideon, maybe you should catch Jacobs before the trial and show your hand. He seems like a straight shooter. Perhaps if you tell him you can prove that Morgan has been using drugs since 1986 and plan to impeach the hell out of him, he'll be willing to waive his claim for emotional distress and punitive damages. That would be a great result, and the risk of the jury giving Morgan a lot of money for lost wages would be minimal."

Gideon knew that Henderson's strategy made some sense. The risk in going to trial in a whistleblower case is that the jury will get angry at the employer and award millions in punitive damages. But Gideon felt that he could hit a home run with his Angel ploy. He thought that Greene would take great delight in seeing Morgan squirm.

"Allen, I'll raise your idea with Ted. But I don't think he'll go with it. He's going to want to try for the knockout, not keep jabbing."

Gideon caught both Greene and McCabe in the hallway before the trial resumed. He advised them of the evening's events. Both were thrilled. He mentioned the idea of trying to force Jacobs' hand before Morgan's cross. Greene rejected it, out of hand.

"Gideon, you should go with your first instinct. We've got to convince the jury that Morgan's a liar. This will do it. I don't want to make any deals."

The bailiff summoned the jury, and the lawyers and parties took their seats at counsel's table. Judge Farmer took the bench at 9:00 a.m. sharp. He thanked the jury for being on time. He asked Gideon if he was ready to proceed with his cross-examination.

"I am, Your Honor," Gideon replied, as Henderson strode quickly to the back of the courtroom. Gideon walked deliberately to the podium and opened the black notebook which contained his cross-examination outline. He would not be using anything in the notebook for a while. This would be pure improvisation.

Henderson opened the back door. In walked Angel. She was wearing bright red. She caught the jury's attention. She caught Morgan's attention. His face turned red.

Q: "Mr. Morgan, you told this jury yesterday that you have not used any drugs since 1986. That is simply untrue, isn't it,

Mr. Morgan?"

"Objection, argumentative," Jacobs howled.

"Withdrawn. I'll rephrase," Gideon responded, savoring the moment. He paused. He looked back toward Angel. He made eye contact with the jury. He paused again.

Q: "Mr. Morgan, isn't it true that you have snorted cocaine since 1986?"

There was a long pause. Morgan wouldn't answer. Jacobs knew something was up. He tried to save his client.

"Your honor, objection as to relevancy. May we have a moment at sidebar?"

A moment at sidebar means that both the lawyers approach the judge and have a conversation among themselves so that the jury cannot hear. It is usually reserved for objections on a critical piece of testimony. The idea is that the parties can state their positions to the judge, get a ruling, and not have the jury prejudiced in any way by the colloquy among counsel.

"Approach, please," Judge Farmer ordered counsel.

"Your honor," Jacobs began, "this is nothing but pure harassment. There is no allegation, and Western Health Corp. cannot prove, that my client ever took drugs while at work. They're trying to taint this trial and prejudice this jury."

Gideon did not even have to respond. Judge Farmer was not buying the argument. "Mr. Jacobs, that's incorrect and you know it. Your client testified that he's been clean since 1986. He opened the door. Mr. Brown is entitled to impeach. Now step back. Objection overruled."

"Mr. Brown, you may re-ask your question," Judge Farmer stated in open court.

"Mr. Morgan, isn't it true that you have snorted cocaine since 1986?"

Morgan again paused. He looked over to Jacobs. Jacobs could offer no more help. He glanced to the back of the courtroom where his father was seating. Jack Morgan was staring straight down at the courtroom tile. Jerry Morgan glared at Angel. Angel sat silently.

"Mr. Morgan, please answer the question," Judge Farmer ordered.

A: "I have used cocaine since 1986. But I was clean my entire time at Western Health Corp., I swear."

Q: "Well, sir, you swore yesterday that you were clean since 1986 and that was untrue, wasn't it?"

A: "I said it was untrue."

Q: "You lied to this jury, didn't you?"

"Objection, argumentative."

"Sustained."

Q: "You used drugs in 1979, isn't that correct?"

A: "Yes."

Q: "You used drugs in 1985 after you left your job as a stock-broker, right?"

A: "I did."

Q: "You have a drug problem, don't you?"

A: "Yes. Yes."

Morgan paused for effect. Angel was whisked out of the court-room. He not only had impeached Morgan, but he had established that Morgan had a drug problem. The jury now knew that Morgan had lied. They would not feel much sympathy for him.

The rest of the cross-examination went smoothly. Morgan was a defeated man on the stand. He caved in on all of Gideon's tough questions. He admitted that he did not know for certain that Marvil was unsafe. He admitted that his productivity had declined in the last year of his job. He admitted that he was absent too much and warned about it. He admitted that his attendance did not improve and that he refused Greene's request to use the employee assistance program.

Gideon did not want to gild the lily. He had gotten all he needed from Morgan. It would still be important to get convincing testimony from Greene, but he was confident Greene would come through. He finished Morgan's cross shortly before the noon lunch break.

Greene was jubilant. "You totally discredited him, Gideon. You were terrific. I think we're well on our way to a defense verdict."

17

There was only one person who could get in the way of Western Health Corp.'s march to victory. But Greene had taken care of that. Ed Miles was conveniently out of the country. He was staying in Greene's country estate in the south of France. Greene did not think that Miles would ever catch on and testify, but he wanted no stone left unturned. Miles would have no incentive to think twice now. Not with a refrigerator stocked with Dom Perignon. Not with Angel on her way on the next Air France flight.

Jacobs would try to throw a wrinkle into Greene's plans after lunch. He would not rest his case, not yet. He would call to the witness stand a Western Health Corp. employee to corroborate Morgan's testimony. He knew he would be in for a battle with Gideon, since the employee did not appear on his witness list and since questions would be asked as to how this employee was contacted. Jacobs would try to dance around that latter issue.

Judge Farmer took the bench promptly at 1:30 p.m. He asked Jacobs to call his next witness. Gideon fully expected to hear that the plaintiff would rest, meaning that Jacobs would not call anymore witnesses, just cross examine Gideon's witnesses.

"Your honor, plaintiff would like to call Stuart Bailey to the

209

stand." Gideon had never heard of Stuart Bailey. He glanced over at Greene. Greene scribbled a note as fast as he could.

"He's one of our employees. Don't let him testify."

Gideon rose quickly to his feet. "Your honor, I request a sidebar before this witness takes the stand."

"Very well, approach," Judge Farmer responded as he motioned counsel to the front of the courtroom.

"Your honor," Gideon began, "I object to this witness being called. He does not appear on the witness list. Mr. Jacobs is trying to sandbag us with a surprise witness, that's what witness lists are supposed to prevent."

"Your honor," Jacobs replied, "this witness was not on our list because he just contacted my office last evening. But he's decided to come forward and has relevant testimony to this case. If Mr. Brown wants a short continuance to prepare his cross, I would certainly have no objection."

"Well, Mr. Brown," Judge Farmer declared, "that certainly seems reasonable. I don't get a sense here that Mr. Jacobs is trying to sandbag you. I am taking him at his word on that. If you feel, after direct examination, that you need extra time to prepare your cross, I will certainly be willing to grant a brief continuance."

Gideon was fuming, but he tried to stay calm and gather his thoughts. Judge Farmer was a fair and reasonable judge. He was probably right that the failure of the witness to appear on the witness list, under these circumstances, should not prevent the witness from testifying.

"Your honor," Gideon resumed after collecting himself. "There is another more troubling issue raised by Mr. Jacobs' attempt to call this witness. And I certainly don't intend to impugn Mr. Jacobs in any way. But regardless of whether Mr. Jacobs initiated the contact, which I hope is not the case, or whether this employee contacted Mr. Jacobs, they have had impermissible *ex parte* communications. The law is clear that employees, current employees of a defendant, who can bind the company with their testimony, may not communicate with opposing counsel on substantive issues. The proper way to elicit such testimony is through a deposition subpoena and through deposition testimony with both sides present."

Judge Farmer was clearly interested in this argument. He did not want to exclude relevant evidence but, on the other hand, he did not want to condone *ex parte* communications between current employees and opposing counsel.

"I view this as a close call, and I don't want to make that call without briefing by the parties. Normally, I would not tolerate any *ex parte* communications of any sort, and I would bar the witness from testifying. But this was not deliberate at all on Mr. Jacobs' part. It appears that the employee came to him and was not solicited by Mr. Jacobs. I suppose he should have informed you of the contact and not have had any substantive discussion with him. Then I could have ordered a deposition and you would have had time to adequately prepare. But he's already talked to him, and that might change my analysis. A deposition probably is not appropriate anymore. Let's get briefing in on this tomorrow afternoon, I'll study the papers tomorrow evening, and I'll make my ruling the next morning."

Gideon was concerned about the testimony, but was pleased that Judge Farmer had given him the opportunity to file a brief. Jacobs' strong point was not legal research or writing, and he felt he would get the best of him in the written argument.

Gideon and Henderson worked late into the night. Together they scoured every case on *ex parte* communications. While such communications were clearly prohibited, Gideon feared that Judge Farmer would want to hear what the testimony was. Gideon had a better idea. He called Jacobs.

"Listen, Bill, I think I'm entitled to know what the general nature of the testimony from Bailey will be. I may not raise a stink if it's something innocuous."

Jacobs was cooperative. "He will verify that Greene and Benczik were having loud arguments. He will corroborate my clients' testimony on this issue. I need to call him to resurrect my clients' credibility."

Gideon thanked Jacobs for his honesty. "Look, I understand you wanting to elicit that testimony, but I'm going to have to oppose you calling this witness. I will tell the judge tomorrow in our papers that we will stipulate that Morgan overheard arguing and that Greene will not deny it on the stand. But that's the best I can do,

Bill."

Jacobs stated that he understood, and that both would make their arguments to Judge Farmer. Gideon again thanked Jacobs for his courtesy, and the two bid each other goodbye.

Gideon had clearly outsmarted Jacobs. He could now take the position that not only were there impermissible *ex parte* communications, but that the testimony sought to be elicited was not controverted. He would argue that Western Health Corp. would be prejudiced if Jacobs was able to put this witness on the stand, after he had already communicated with him. Gideon knew that Judge Farmer was not that impressed with this testimony anyhow and would now not feel he was excluding relevant evidence.

Gideon was right. Judge Farmer ruled that the witness could not testify because there had been *ex parte* communications. He further ruled that if he had been inclined to make an exception and let the witness testify, he no longer felt so inclined because the subject of the testimony was not disputed. Jacobs really could not argue strenuously with Judge Farmer's reasoning, since he was concerned anyhow with how Jack Morgan had found out about the witness and feared something might come out on cross. Gideon, on the other hand, had dodged a major bullet.

18

Jack Morgan was livid when he heard the judge's ruling. He felt that Judge Farmer was hurting his son's case. He had to get Jacobs some evidence, even if it meant waiting until rebuttal.

Jack Morgan telephoned Gonzales from the payphone in the courtroom hallway. He pleaded with Gonzales to get some more information about the dispute between Greene and Benczik. And what about Benczik's murder?

Although the police suspected his son, Jack knew that Jerry was incapable of committing murder. Jerry had sworn to both Jack and Jacobs that he was not involved in the murder. It had to have been done by Greene, or one of his henchmen, Jack Morgan thought. If he could only get some type of evidence to prove his theory, it would blow the case wide open.

Gonzales told Morgan that there was only one thing left to do. He would break into Ted Greene's office late that evening. He had heard that Greene had a locked desk drawer where he kept all his secret papers. Perhaps he could find something, anything, to help Morgan win his case.

Neither Jack Morgan nor Gonzales had heard the clicking noise while they were on the line. Neither knew that the phone was tapped. Their little conversation was not a secret anymore. The conversation would be reported immediately to the boss. The boss would not be happy to hear about Gonzales' plan. He would no doubt take action, decisive action.

19

Judge Farmer took the bench, and the trial resumed. Jacobs was asked to call his next witness. Jacobs advised the judge that the plaintiff would rest. This meant that it was now time for Gideon to put on the case for the defense and to call Western Health Corp.'s witnesses.

The first witness Gideon wanted to present to the jury was Benczik. Benczik, of course, could not give live testimony. Instead, Gideon planned to read portions of the deposition to the jury. Henderson would go to the witness stand and play Benczik's role in answering the questions.

Gideon and Henderson had rehearsed the reading of the deposition on a number of occasions. Henderson dressed the part. He wore a conservative gray suit. He had a neatly trimmed haircut, which he slicked down with Vitalis. He wore wire rimmed glasses. Except for the age difference, he looked remarkably like Benczik. The jury might even believe that he was a scientist.

Gideon had carefully chosen the parts of the deposition to be read before the jury. He wanted to keep the testimony relatively short, so that he would not lose the jury's attention. It was important, though, to read all of the part about Benczik's background and training. Gideon wanted the jury to think Benczik was smart and would have detected any flaw in Marvil, if there was one.

The deposition reading went as well as could be expected. While Gideon would have preferred to have the real Alex Benczik on the stand, the jury appeared to listen to all the testimony. Many of them took notes.

It took about two hours to read to the jury the relevant portions of Benczik's deposition testimony, including a twenty-minute break after the first hour. When Gideon and Henderson concluded, Judge Farmer asked Jacobs if there was any portion of the deposition that he would like to read to the jury. There really was very little in the deposition for Jacobs to emphasize; he therefore declined to read any of it to the jury.

The judge recessed the trial for lunch. The defense team prepared their strategy for the rest of the trial. Ben Williams, Morgan's former supervisor, would be called to the witness stand in the afternoon. His testimony and cross would take the rest of the day. Greene would be the main attraction the next day. Gideon fully expected Greene to be on direct examination for most of the day. Greene had been extremely well prepped. His testimony would be devastating.

The mood on the other side of the cafeteria where Jacobs and the Morgan's were having lunch was somber. They had only presented the slimmest of evidence. Barring a major screw up by Greene, the jury would be hard pressed to find for Morgan, especially because Gideon had caught Morgan lying to the jury about his drug use.

Jack Morgan contributed little to the conversation. He did not want to tip off Jacobs about Gonzales' game plan. Jacobs would throw a fit. He was worried enough about meeting with the Western Health Corp. employees. He would never condone an operative rifling through Ted Greene's locked drawers.

As lunch ended, McCabe, who had watched most of the trial, offered his first words of encouragement to Gideon in front of Greene. "Gideon, you've got the jury in the palm of your hand. They trust you, not Morgan or Jacobs. At the beginning of the case, you told the jury that they would not keep their promises, and then you caught Morgan in a bold-faced lie. They trust you, Gideon. Just ride through the rest of the testimony in the same fashion. Don't try to prove too much. The only way they win is if they can catch us lying, and they can't."

Gideon was surprised by the praise heaped upon him by McCabe, especially in front of a client. It was rare for compliments to be given to associates of Longworth & Drucker at all, much less in front of such an important client as Ted Greene. McCabe was finally sharing some of the credit.

"Look," McCabe continued, "I'm going to bug out early today and take care of a few matters. Ted, of course I'll be here first thing tomorrow to hear the star witness bring this thing home."

Greene and McCabe exchanged a handshake, and McCabe

headed out of the courthouse. The rest walked back to Judge Farmer's courtroom. Williams was ready to go. He had been good in preparation; his answers were clear and succinct.

Williams' testimony was masterful. Sometimes, the witness you most fear is the star at trial; other times the witness you think the jury would love fails miserably. Williams had clearly surprised all. He told the jury, with conviction, all the performance problems that Morgan had and all the efforts he made to assist Morgan with his performance.

The jury was impressed with the level of detail in his performance reviews of Morgan, and in the written warnings prepared by Williams. While Jacobs was able to poke a hole here and there about a few minor details, the Morgans were plainly forlorn at the close of the day. The one witness who could put his foot in his mouth, the one witness who they thought might fold under pressure, was too well coached to trip up.

They could only imagine what Ted Greene had in store for them the next morning.

20

Gonzales stayed at Western Health Corp. late, sorting the mail. He waited until all the employees had left. There was not another light on in the whole place. Gonzales was alone.

He walked around the hallway again just to make sure. He looked behind all the closed doors. He was sure it was safe.

Ted Greene's door was always locked. Picking it would be no trouble whatsoever for Gonzales. He was able to open the door in no time at all.

Gonzales headed straight to Ted Greene's desk. That lock was a little trickier. It took Gonzales some time to open it.

There were piles of papers in the drawer. Gonzales read through each one carefully. None of the papers related to Marvil. They all pertained to various investments that Greene had made through the years. Ted Greene was certainly a wealthy man. His stock portfolio was astonishing.

Gonzales was about to give up when he came across one final stack at the bottom of the drawer. Again, it looked like more of Greene's brokerage statements. He noticed one sheet of lined paper in the stack that stuck out a bit. He pulled out the sheet of paper. There were handwritten notes on it. The notes were in pencil. He saw the word "Marvil" written on it.

He read no further. This time the murder would be clean and swift. He attacked Gonzales from behind. Gonzales never had a chance. A rope was placed firmly around his neck. He pulled it as tightly as he could. Gonzales struggled valiantly for a moment. But he was quick to succumb.

There would be no blood. There would be no body found. He had confiscated a mail sack used to deliver Western Health Corp.'s mail. It was just big enough for Gonzales' body. Before leaving, he placed the documents Gonzales was reading back into the drawer. He locked the drawer securely.

The body was carried down the back stairway. It wasn't far from the stairwell to the car. He opened the trunk and lifted the body into it. He drove up the canyon to a deserted part of the Santa Monica mountains. He dumped the body out. By the time some poor hiker would find it, the coyotes would have all but devoured it.

21

"Your honor, the defense calls Ted Greene to the stand," Gideon stated confidently in front of the jury. Greene stood up at counsel table and strode proudly to the witness stand. He raised his right arm and took the oath. He sat down and awaited Gideon's questions. The jury was mesmerized.

He was the perfect witness. He answered questions in a relaxed and conversational manner. He exuded warmth. He was dashingly handsome, and the jury, eight of them women, no doubt was charmed by him. He was larger than life.

Gideon had Greene first go into his background. The jury heard about Greene's unparalleled rise to success. Graduated college at 22. Finished business school at 24. Worked his way up to president of Western Health Corp. by the age of 36. Was named CEO of the year the last two years. His company had developed drugs that were revolutionizing the medical field, and he was hopeful that they might market a drug within the next several years which would combat the HIV virus.

Gideon had Greene explain to the jury how he ran the company. There was a commitment to excellence. Everybody had to carry his weight. There was no slacking off. Those who worked hard and were committed to the company were paid handsomely. Even starting salaries were well above the industry standard. The company was committed to diversity in its hiring practices; in fact, it had recently been recognized in a business journal for its hiring and promotion of women and minorities.

The jury was listening attentively to Greene. No doubt many of them wished that they worked for a man like Ted Greene. It was also no coincidence that Gideon had selected eight women and four minorities for the jury.

Gideon then began to probe Western Health Corp's history in the drug field.

Q: "You've been at Western Health Corp. how long, Mr. Greene?"

A: "It's been over seventeen years now."

Q: "And how many drugs would you estimate Western Health Corp. has developed over that time?"

A: "We must have developed three or four dozen different drugs. But we don't try to market every drug we develop. We subject the drug to rigorous testing. If there is even the slightest question about the drug, we drop it. Every drug we have chosen to submit to the FDA has gotten their approval, including Marvil."

Q: "Was there ever any question in your mind whatsoever, sir, about the safety of Marvil?"

A: "Absolutely not. If there was, I would not have let it go to the FDA, that I can assure you," Greene responded, looking directly at the jury.

Gideon put before Greene a number of documents from the FDA approval process. Greene explained all the tests that were conducted, and the rigorous review undertaken by the FDA. He stated passionately that there was not even a single test, not one, which raised any question about the safety of Marvil.

Gideon then shifted his focus to Jerry Morgan.

Q: "Now, Ted, you sat in this courtroom and heard Mr. Morgan explain why he thought he was fired. Was his testimony true?"

A: "There is simply not a grain of truth to it. Ben Williams, his supervisor, tried everything in his power to help Morgan succeed. You have heard him testify about these efforts. Mr. Williams reported to me almost daily about his efforts. The plain fact is that Mr. Morgan did not meet our standards. And I admit that they are tough. But that is why we've been as successful as we have been. That is why we're going to beat the HIV virus."

Q: "At any time, prior to the time that you discharged Mr. Morgan, did you know that he thought anything about Marvil was unsafe?"

A: "No, of course not. Had Mr. Morgan complained, I would have taken it seriously and reported it to the FDA. I would have insisted that they do a follow-up investigation. If there were any questions, we would have pulled the drug. In fact, after I learned about Mr. Morgan's concerns through this lawsuit, the FDA was contacted, and they reviewed all their files. And once again they found absolutely nothing wrong with Marvil."

Q: "Now, Mr. Greene, what about this conversation between you and Mr. Benczik that Mr. Morgan has testified about?"

A: "Mr. Morgan did overhear a conversation between Mr. Benczik and me. And I did raise my voice at one point. But, I swear, that conversation had nothing to do with any concerns about the safety of Marvil. Quite the contrary. I was urging Mr. Benczik to work incredibly long hours because I wanted to be sure, absolutely sure, that Marvil was completely safe before we marketed it. I wanted him to work around the clock with the FDA investigators, share all of our test results, so that we would be sure the drug was as revolutionary as we thought it was."

The jury was riveted. Gideon paused for effect. He would ask just one more question.

Q: "Mr. Greene, would you share with the jury what the FDA told you about Marvil when it concluded its investigation?"

"Objection, hearsay," Jacobs bristled.

"It's not hearsay, your honor, the FDA officials are in Washington, D.C., and are beyond the subpoena power of this court. They are hence unavailable, and the testimony can come in," Gideon countered.

"I'll allow it," Judge Farmer responded.

This was one last chance to let Western Health Corp. toot its own horn. Gideon would let Greene have his moment in the sun.

A: "They thanked us for all the help we had given them. They said they had never seen such rigorous testing and files in such order. They even remarked that they could not believe that Benczik and I kept such detailed notes, notes of literally every discussion. And I'll never forget what the investigator said when he walked out the door after giving final approval to Marvil. It was very touching. He said that his sister had suffered bouts of depression for years, and nothing helped her without producing terrible side effects. And he said that he wanted to be the first person to buy Marvil, and he took out his wallet to pay for a prescription. I, of course, wouldn't accept his money."

Gideon told the judge that he had no further questions. Jacobs had a strained look on his face. Greene had put the nail in the coffin. He had left no opening. Jacobs admirably poked around on cross, scoring a point here and there. But it was much too little too late. There was no doubt in anyone's mind that the jury would issue a defense verdict. There was no doubt in Gideon's mind what that would mean for his career at Longworth & Drucker; he would certainly make partner after winning the most important case in the history of the labor department.

Gideon was too excited to go home after court. He went back to the office. He kept replaying the day's events in his mind. He knew that Greene would be a superb witness, but he never dreamed that he would be that good. And that last bit of testimony was the kicker. He was sure that Greene had embellished the story somewhat. He had never heard Greene mention in preparation the bit about how great Benczik's and Greene's notes were. But there was no harm in being a bit theatrical in front of the jury.

And then Gideon had a sickening thought. NOTES. Greene and Benczik did keep notes of everything. He had read them all ten times. But why in hell were there not any notes of the conversation that Morgan overheard between Benczik and Greene? Especially given that Greene had seen Morgan after the conversation? Where the fuck were the notes?

22

Gideon was beside himself. He had to find out the answer. There must be some rational explanation.

He picked up the phone to call Greene. The phone rang ten times. Greene was not in the office. He must have gone straight home. Gideon did not want to bother Greene at home.

Well, he had a key. Greene had given it to him at the start of the case. He had told Gideon that he could use it anytime that he wanted. Surely, there was nothing wrong about using it now. If Greene somehow made it back to the office, he would just tell him that he was reviewing everything one last time, to make sure that they had left no stone untouched, to make sure that they didn't need to call or recall any witnesses before the defense rested.

He grabbed the key and headed for the parking garage. He got into his little red sportscar and sped up the freeway. It was 8:00 p.m.

His heart was pounding. There had to be some explanation. He felt like Dustin Hoffman in The Graduate, speeding up the coast in his red Alfa Romeo, rushing to stop Elaine's marriage. But this was somehow much more serious.

How could he not have been given a document, notes, about

the most critical conversation in the whole case? He thanked his lucky stars that Jacobs had not picked up on the fact that there were no notes of the conversation. He could have made a big deal about it in front of the jury.

It was just about 9:00 p.m. when he arrived at Western Health Corp. The place was dark, unlike Longworth & Drucker at that hour. The front door was locked. He inserted the key. It worked. He entered Western Health Corp.

He went up the elevator to Ted Greene's floor. All the documents were kept in his office – Alex Benczik had told him so. The originals of all of the documents were locked in the file cabinet. Ted Greene had let him know that.

Gideon opened Greene's door and headed straight to the file cabinet. There were boxes and boxes of documents in it. He would spend all night, if necessary, going through every document.

He was in the office for hours. There was no document that Gideon had not seen before. These were the originals of the copies Greene had sent to him, just as Greene said. He was beginning to feel foolish. Maybe Greene and Benczik simply didn't make notes of the conversation. It was an innocent conversation. Perhaps there just wasn't anything to make note of.

He was about to leave, to go home. He was embarrassed for believing the worst. Ali's skepticism about the case had gotten to him. His imagination was running wild.

He caught the desk drawer out of the corner of his eye. It was locked. He had to know. He had not driven all the way up there and spent hours looking through all the documents to leave with any doubt. The key did not open the drawer. He was terrible at anything mechanic. How would he pry it open?

He tried to open the drawer for what seemed like hours. He finally took a letter opener from Greene's desk and stuck it into the side of the drawer. He pressed as hard as he could. The lock sprung open.

He was speed reading through document after document. They were all about Greene's financial investments.

Gideon felt like he was prying. He was ashamed. But he read on.

He came to the bottom stack. He thought he heard a noise in the hallway. Must just be his imagination.

He came to the handwritten document. It was in pencil. He had seen this handwriting before. He could not believe his eyes.

"Mtg. T. Greene, A. Benczik, B. McCabe. Discussed Marvil and FDA. Benczik concerned. A couple rats died. Greene thinks too late now. I concur. It's part of the business."

Gideon was stunned. It had all been a charade. McCabe had been involved from the beginning. He knew that Benczik had concerns about Marvil. He had "concurred" with Greene to cover it up. No doubt he probably advised Greene to get rid of Morgan once they thought he had overheard the conversation.

Ali was right. She was always right. The story was just too

good to be true. How could he not have seen the handwriting on the wall?

Suddenly, a bunch of little things began to make sense. Why Benczik was a little bit upset when Gideon had made mincemeat out of Morgan during the deposition. Why Greene decided at the last moment to be present during Benczik's deposition. Surely, Benczik wouldn't fold in front of his boss. So Benczik knew the truth, he wanted to tell somebody. So, he calls Ali of all people, he'd never even met her. But maybe he thinks she'll alert me, that I'll put two and two together. Little does he know that I'm just too immersed in the case to see the light. Then he calls McCabe. That's why he calls McCabe. He had met him before. McCabe was in the goddamn room and knew all. He was asking McCabe to reconsider. He shuddered to think what McCabe had told Benczik.

McCabe and Greene had asked Benczik to suborn perjury. Gideon couldn't believe it. Two men who he trusted.

Gideon had an even more sickening thought. One, or maybe both, of them had murdered Benczik. Oh, my god. He would have to tell the police about it.

At that moment, McCabe entered Greene's office. McCabe was calm and collected.

"So now you know, Gideon, you're too good a lawyer not to have found out sooner or later. But of course, that's why I wanted you to do the trial, because you're a good lawyer."

Gideon was speechless. McCabe was all but confessing to

231

counseling a client to commit perjury, and maybe to more.

"Bart, did Western Health Corp.'s business mean that much to you, for Christ sake? Benczik tells you that he has doubts, and you tell him to shut up, to keep it under the table?"

"Look, Gideon, you're in the big leagues here. This is a multi-million-dollar account. Do you know what that means for Longworth & Drucker profits? We're all going to benefit, Gideon, even you, you'll see it in your profit-sharing checks when you are made partner."

So, there it was. Blackmail. McCabe was holding out the carrot. Keep quiet, be a good trooper, win the case, you'll be a partner.

It was 3:00 a.m. when he got home. Ali was asleep. He wanted to talk with her. She would give him courage to do the right thing.

It was useless; he had to make the decision himself. He knew where Ali stood. Expose Greene. Expose McCabe. The hell with your career. You work too hard anyway. So what if McCabe ruins your career?

Gideon did not sleep a wink. He got to the office at 7:00 a.m. Maybe he would talk to Henderson. Henderson would have the answer. He buzzed Allen on the phone. Allen came to Gideon's office. He told him the whole sordid story.

Henderson told Gideon to be true to himself, that the firm wasn't worth it, that he should call McCabe's bluff. He thought maybe McCabe would fold. Gideon knew, however, that McCabe would fight all the way.

"Bart, I'm going to take this to Judge Farmer, tomorrow. We knowingly withheld a document that we had an ethical obligation to turn over to the other side."

But McCabe had anticipated this. He had not gone to Harvard law school and became head of L&D's labor department by being outsmarted.

"Don't be silly, Gideon, my notes are privileged. It's confidential attorney-client privilege. You can't tell Judge Farmer, and if you do, I am prepared to convince him that it should not come into evidence."

McCabe wasn't entirely right; you cannot counsel a client to commit perjury on concealed evidence. But Gideon knew McCabe would argue like hell to the judge. He could well ruin Gideon's career. Certainly, partnership at Longworth & Drucker would be out of the question.

He picked up the phone to call Jacobs. Maybe he could leak the information to Jacobs. Jacobs could get out a subpoena for all notes of the conversation. Maybe, at least, Western Health Corp. would settle.

He never got a chance to talk to Jacobs. McCabe stormed into his office. He told Henderson to get out. He hung up Gideon's phone.

"Let's go down to the courthouse and get this over with. I'll accompany you. I'm sure that you won't try anything stupid."

Gideon's mind raced as he entered the courthouse. He had a

decision to make. The jury was summoned to the courtroom. Judge Farmer took the bench.

Gideon of the Bible was the courageous warrior portrayed in Judges. With a small band of 300, he drove out of Israel a huge, oppressive force of idolatrous Midianities. Would Gideon Brown sound the trumpet like his Biblical predecessors?

"Mr. Brown, you may proceed," Judge Farmer stated.

Gideon got up slowly from counsel's table. He legs wobbled. He was short of breath.

"Your honor," Gideon said slowly, "THE DEFENSE RESTS."

EPILOGUE

His alarm went off louder than necessary at 7:00 a.m. He flicked the switch on the radio off and put his head back on the pillow. He snoozed until about 7:30 a.m. He showered, shaved and gave his half-asleep wife a peck on the cheek as he headed out the door.

He arrived at work at 8:30 a.m. As usual, the message light on the phone was flashing. He had one message. "See me as soon as you get in, I've got a new case I want you to handle."

He grabbed a cup of coffee on his way to the partner's office. The door was shut. He knocked on the door and peeked in. Gideon was on the phone, as usual, but waved Henderson in. Gideon had yet to make eye contact with him when he pushed a document in front of Henderson. It was a Complaint filed in Superior Court.

ACKNOWLEDGEMENTS

I write this book in memory of my dad, Artie Horowitz (10/24/25 - 4/23/2017), and my son, Jake (12/11/95 - 8/6/17).

I dedicate this book to my mom, Shirley Horowitz, who just turned 92. She instilled in me the love of writing and the attempt to find the perfect word.

I wish to thank my daughter, Nicole Horowitz, for giving me the courage to finish this book. This may be the longest time in history a book was written. I started it in 2001 while still at the big Los Angeles law firm, O'Melveny & Myers. When I left O'Melveny in August 2002, I spent my six weeks off after some visits back East to my parents and family, typing this book on my in-law's computer at their house. This was before computers were in every household, and we did not have one. I never finished the book but tried again in the late 2000's, only to put it down to publish my first book, "Row 47." Just a few months ago Nicole told me to finish it, and I did. This is my first book of fiction and legal thriller. Thank you, Nicole.

Made in the USA
Middletown, DE
17 December 2022

18829822R00142